The Pillow Case Murders

Brian Grant

CW00820546

To Sally for her patience, Oliver for his artistic and IT help, Rory for always being supportive, and Melissa for her enthusiasm and assistance.

Cover Designed by Oliver Grant

ISBN: 9798710062944

PUBLISH**NATION**
www.publishnation.co.uk

Chapter One

Henry Hetherington-Busby was sweating profusely. 'I'm getting a bit old for this sort of thing,' he thought, as beads of perspiration fell on to the pillow. The woman below him was thrashing her legs about with an impressive vigour that belied her age and her stifled moans were getting louder. 'For God's sake keep the noise down,' thought Henry; 'you'll wake up everyone in the building.' His prayers were answered as with one last involuntary convulsion she sank back on to the mattress. Henry remained on top of her for a few moments until his breathing had become calmer. He slid off and stared at her motionless body which now seemed very frail after the exertions of the last few minutes. As he recovered he felt both elation and a little anxiety. He removed the pillow from her face and felt her pulse. Yes, six days before her seventy-ninth birthday, Sophie Delouche had definitely had her last bedroom encounter. He looked at her eyes staring at the ceiling, still registering shock and alarm.

'Died in her sleep,' murmured Henry. A smile crossed his lips. 'The things I do for mother.'

Henry's transformation from inoffensive and mild mannered accountant to heartless killer had been remarkably quick, and was the consequence of a sudden and unforeseen change in his circumstances. Bunty Hetherington-Busby was losing her marbles. This was not the medical diagnosis, but in layman's terms she and the plot were parting company, and the distance between them was increasing at an alarming rate. A nursing home was the obvious solution but his mother was as healthy as nursing homes were expensive. It didn't take Henry long to realise that the inheritance he had been looking forward to would evaporate if she lived to a ripe old age in a nursing home. So, after a candid discussion with his reluctant wife Audrey, the Hetherington-Busbys decided to do the decent thing and take mother in. After all, how much trouble could an eighty-two year old widow be?

1

To a more intuitive man than Henry, little clues might have served as a warning of disappointments to come. He felt sure that her solicitor had mentioned her debenture when discussing her move to Winkford over the phone.

'He said she's got dementia you idiot,' Audrey had shrieked at him. 'It's a bloody disease. She can't remember what she did yesterday.'

Henry remained positive. How bad could that be?

Bunty Hetherington-Busby's father had been in the Foreign Office and her mother had baked cakes. Her employment as a PA at Hampton Jeffrey, the largest firm of accountants in Winkford, was due more to the influence of her father, a close friend of one of the senior partners, than to her intellect. She had secured her position within the firm by availing her managers of what became known as a Bunty Bonus. This unusual perk at HJ ended her already fractious relationship with her father and resulted in Henry having practically no contact with his grandparents. When Audrey met Henry she was the receptionist at a small firm of undertakers. Henry was a junior accountant arranging the funeral of his grandparents who had died while hill walking in Scotland. Hilda Hetherington-Busby had fallen from the Clachaig Gully path in Glencoe while experiencing one of her dizzy spells. She had instinctively grabbed her husband's arm for support, taking him with her. Henry had little contact with them in life but was now charged with arranging their funeral. He lacked confidence and came to rely on the quiet but approachable Audrey to help him through the process. Mother's decision to take up residence in her parents substantial home in Ealing, which she now owned, meant that Henry was able to pursue a girl whom his mother saw as far below their social standing and 'lacking sparkle'. Bunty forgot Winkford almost as soon as she left and abandoned Henry just as quickly. She came to their wedding three years later, and after a good soaking in champagne, let it be known to all and sundry that Henry, 'could have done better'. Audrey consoled herself with the knowledge that while she came from a happy, stable home, Henry was the son of an unmarried mother and had no idea who his father was. His childhood had left him scarred. A tubby child, he had been bullied at school, had a singular fear of snakes, and had invented a fictitious father who was on the wrong side of the law. For the most part, Bunty remained out of their lives, Henry's career was progressing slowly, and they were moving up Winkford's social ladder. Audrey was content with her lot. She had to remain pleasant to Mother on the rare occasions that they spoke on the phone because the house in Ealing was now seen as their pension plan. Suddenly the pension had to be earned and she would have to become Mother's carer. Audrey wasn't happy but Henry was confident that her underlying decency would prevail.

Mother's move to the home of her son and daughter-in-law in mid-June was straightforward and uneventful, which boded well for the future. Henry had restricted her to three suitcases and a small box of mementoes, and she took up residence in the double room at the top of the stairs. It wasn't large but had the benefit of its own ensuite. Audrey would bring a cup of tea and toast to Mother's room every morning and explain to her where she was. By mid-September she had to explain to mother who she was, and Audrey was finding Winkford's equivalent of Ground Hog Day more than a bit wearing.

Then there was the problem of her friends and siblings not phoning her any more. Short of employing a psychic, this wasn't going to happen as they had all taken up residence in the church grounds; six feet under the church grounds to be precise. Just once Audrey had tried to explain to her that they were all dead, and she still broke into a sweat when she recalled the emotional carnage that had followed. Mother's extraordinary outpouring of grief had necessitated a visit from the local GP to sedate her.

'All of them,' she had kept repeating in horror. 'All of them. What had happened? How had it happened? When had it happened? Why wasn't it reported in the news? Why hadn't she been told?' With every comforting lie, the story that evolved became more implausible. The carnage which befell the sleepy village of Upper Bentley just kept on escalating. Some of mother's friends lived there. Others just happened to be visiting. The really unlucky ones were merely driving through when disaster struck. Then there were the ones on the flight; wrong day; wrong flight. The fateful day when a jumbo jet fell from the sky onto Upper Bentley was never mentioned again. The following day mother had again pointed out that she hadn't heard from Dotty Henderson among others. As she was quick to point out, it wasn't surprising that they didn't contact her. They probably didn't know where she was. After all she wasn't that sure herself, and she never contacted them. Audrey promised to get their phone numbers. Remarkably, this was one piece of information that mother could somehow always remember and Audrey found herself in the frustrating position of having to explain her own apparent lapses of memory.

However, the major problem wasn't what she forgot; it was what she remembered from her distant, and it appeared colourful, past. Who was Jack Beveridge? Why did she keep talking about him as though she'd seen him only yesterday and constantly refer to him as Donkey Jack, a nickname which had led Audrey to assume he was either a few cards short of a full deck or had an I.Q. of room temperature. Not only that, she felt the need to enquire about him at the most inappropriate of times and in the most inappropriate company. Her reference to him at their dinner party in October, with the friends they had taken years to acquire as they 'moved up the food chain', to quote Audrey, had been particularly embarrassing. Air Commodore Andrew's wife had raised a chuckle when she asked quite innocently why he had been called Donkey, but mother's calm reply had been quite appalling and had stunned the table. The silence which followed was as pregnant as Phyllis Thornton, and she was having difficulty reaching her lemonade and orange. Henry's usually agile brain seemed to have frozen and it was Audrey who asked in a loud voice if anyone had done a bungee jump. The sense of relief was palpable as all present enthusiastically informed the table that they had not, had never considered it, and had no intention of ever doing so. Audrey saw every face around the table turn expectantly towards her. She explained that she shared their lack of enthusiasm and

4

hadn't done one either. The silence which followed was broken by Mother asking if anyone had seen Dotty Henderson recently.

It was around this time that the issue of Power of Attorney presented itself for consideration. With the deterioration in her mental state it seemed appropriate to put her care on a proper legal footing and sell the house in Ealing. It was at this point that the true state of Mother's finances came to light. It appeared that she had been indulging herself on the finer things in life for years. Since the death of Henry's grandparents she had acquired a taste for fine dining, expensive champagne, and a group of affluent friends with similar tastes. Mother had been at the top of her social ladder while Henry and Audrey were still in sight of the bottom rung of theirs. If any consideration of her son's inheritance had crossed her mind it had been a fleeting thought between mouthfuls of Dom Perignon champagne. She had extracted a large percentage of the capital from her home when the money had begun to dwindle and First Regal Finance was now the major shareholder in the property. Audrey was struggling to find something, anything, to like about the relentlessly demanding and constantly embarrassing mother-in-law from hell whom she had unwillingly adopted. Henry had to break the news that most of the inheritance that they had been anticipating had been squandered on cocktails, truffles, and designer labels. Audrey did not take the news well.

As Audrey drove up to the house, she immediately knew that something was wrong. The clue was in the smoke wafting through the open kitchen window. Slamming on the brakes, she ran to the kitchen and smothered the flames leaping from the pan with a wet towel. She rushed to the lounge where mother was deeply engrossed in day time television.

'Why did you turn on the hob?' she screamed at her. Mother appeared flustered at first and then completely bewildered, but her expression quickly changed and she became perfectly lucid.

'We don't appear to have any Babycham and Dotty is popping round for a catch up this afternoon. Could you get some ginger syrup while you're at it?'

5

She turned her attention back to the television and laughed out loud at the reminiscences of a B-List celebrity.

Audrey realised that she had been dismissed. She walked into the kitchen, stared at the fridge, and screamed. She retrieved her phone from her handbag and phoned Henry at the office.

Henry listened in silence to Audrey's calm and measured ultimatum. 'She's got to go. She can't be left on her own and I don't intend to become a prisoner in this house. In the meantime we'll have to get someone to babysit her when I have to go out. If she doesn't go, and go soon, I'll be the one that goes, and believe me, that will cost you a lot more than a nursing home.'

'But where can we put her?' asked Henry.

'Put her down a bloody mine shaft for all I care,' was her shrill response. Her voice was no longer calm and measured and Henry knew that mother was going into a home.

Chapter Two

After years of slowly 'working their way up the food chain', Henry was now counting the cost. Only one nursing home was acceptable. Morderton Manor Retirement Home in Winkford was exclusively for the upper end of the social spectrum, and the price tag kept it that way. Overlooking Lincombe Park Golf Course, it was an imposing building with an aura of opulence. Henry and Audrey drove to Morderton Manor in silence. As they entered the grounds they saw the three storey, eighteenth century building for the first time. They, like everyone before them, were impressed. It was the legacy of Joshua Nutley, a Victorian clock manufacturer and philanthropist. He had built it as a home for those who, like his beloved mother, had been diagnosed as clinically insane but received little sympathy or understanding from the bulk of humanity. Those working with the dementia patients on the first floor were prone to wonder sometimes if much had changed.

With the typical black humour of the times, Joshua Nutley's home for the clinically insane was quickly abbreviated from Nutley House to The Nut House, and was referred to as such throughout the nineteenth century. The name was eventually changed to Morderton Manor, honouring a local dignitary whose accomplishments, if any, were long forgotten.

Morderton Manor had been adopted by the state with the advent of the National Health Service. Further changes to mental health provision had led to its inmates being dispersed and it being sold to the private sector.

With a huge investment in its refurbishment Morderton Manor became a five star retirement and nursing home, and the penultimate destination of the most affluent people in the county.

The car park was at the bottom of the drive and to the left of the building from where the landscaped grounds and imposing building were shown to maximum advantage. Imposing it was. Henry and Audrey sat in the car and stared at it for several minutes. The grass had the carpet like finish found on the best golf courses and it could have been a giant green had it not been for the conifers which rose majestically from it at irregular intervals. A border of colourful bushes, of which they only recognised the rhododendrons, confirmed the sense of opulence that the garden exuded. The building itself had an impressive tower at each end and a large clock above the main entrance, but its most striking characteristic was the rows of high windows which surrounded all three floors at regular intervals.

'Can we afford to send her here?' Audrey asked in an incredulous voice.

'Can we afford not to?' Henry replied as he thought of their hard won place in Winkford society.

They made their way to the large wooden door, rang the bell, and gave their names through the intercom as requested. After a few moments the door opened and they entered.

As they stepped into the deep pile of the dark blue carpet their eyes were immediately drawn to the large crystal chandelier hanging from the ceiling. Behind a row of plush sofas and marble coffee tables, fitted dark oak bookcases adorned the wall. If the décor had been designed to impress, it had succeeded. The reception area could have been the foyer of a luxury hotel.

A pleasant young receptionist standing behind the desk looked up from her computer screen, informed them that Mrs Lloyd-King would be along shortly, and offered them a cup of tea. They declined and smiled at the only other occupant in the room, a smartly dressed if somewhat severe older woman who ignored them. The phone rang, and after a hushed conversation the young receptionist left, flashing a beaming smile in their direction.

'She won't be here for much longer,' the other woman said.

'Oh really,' replied Henry somewhat mystified. 'Is she moving on?'

'She certainly is. She doesn't know it yet but she'll be gone by the end of the month.'

Henry and Audrey made no comment but the woman appeared eager to share her displeasure with them.

'I've been here for over half an hour and have I been offered a cup of tea? No, I have not. Well if she thinks there won't be repercussions, she's mistaken. She's just resigned as far as I'm concerned.'

Henry felt a little uncomfortable with the direction of the conversation.

'She seems to be a very pleasant young woman and I'm sure it was just an oversight,' he ventured.

'An oversight,' she replied scornfully. 'Well it's one oversight too many. It's not the first time it's happened.'

Henry steered the conversation into calmer waters. 'Do you visit Morderton Manor often,' he enquired.

She looked at him with an expression of incredulity.

'Visit,' she said. 'Visit isn't the term I would use. I own this establishment. I don't expect to be treated with disrespect by a jumped-up little secretary with ideas above her station.'

Henry was genuinely dumbfounded.

'I didn't realise,' Well I wouldn't, would I? It's a beautiful nursing home you have here,' he added, determined to lighten the atmosphere. 'My mother's going to be staying here shortly.'

The woman ignored his intervention and continued to vent her displeasure with relish.

'All this unemployment and we end up with little strumpets who don't even show common courtesy to the woman who pays their wages. Well, we'll see how she fares in the job market with the reference I'm going to give her.'

She was warming to her theme, but at this point the young woman returned to reception still smiling and obviously totally oblivious to the feelings of her employer towards her.

An awkward silence followed until a uniformed member of the nursing staff strode up to the woman and took her by the hand.

'This is where you've been hiding, Mrs Thompson. It's time for your morning tea break and your pills. Your son is taking you to the garden centre for lunch today so we'll get you dressed in something less formal. I know how much you enjoy his visits.'

The woman suddenly looked much more subdued as she followed the carer out of the room without as much as a backward glance.

Henry looked at Audrey. Neither spoke but they shared a troubling premonition of Mother's future.

A few minutes later Mrs Lloyd-King swept into the room, charming and sophisticated, but with a steeliness in her smile which alluded to a ruthless streak. After polite introductions she led them to her office where she gave a commendable sales pitch, slipping in the considerable cost as though of no consequence. Henry and Audrey were then passed on to one of her staff, a middle aged woman named Sylvia, who gave them a guided tour of the crème de la crème of luxury living for those in their twilight years.

The first floor was the Dementia Unit, and this was where Mother would be staying. The rooms were definitely five star, as was the communal area. Only accessible by lifts, one had to know the code to access them. 123 had been cracked by a combination of luck and its simple sequence, so the code had been changed to 132. This ensured that the first floor combination would not be hacked by its residents again and was completely secure.

'Even if they see it being used it isn't a problem,' Sylvia explained. 'Few of them would remember it.'

The residents on the ground and third floors were for the most part both intelligent and lucid. They rarely had contact with those residing in what they referred to affectionately as La La land. Sylvia was proving to be surprisingly insensitive. Audrey enquired why this unit was on the first floor.

'We've learnt a few lessons from Colditz,' she chuckled. 'No tunnels here.'

There was air conditioning and the windows which overlooked the golf course were always locked. After all, as Sylvia explained, one couldn't have one of the old dears reliving their first parachute jump on to the petunias one floor below.

Henry and Audrey found themselves sitting opposite Mrs Lloyd-King again, and Henry was eager to cut to the chase and

10

get the ball rolling. He thanked her for the tour, enthused briefly about how impressed they both were, and asked when mother could move in.

'Well that's not easy to predict,' said Mrs Lloyd-King. 'We are full at present, and she would have to reside in a room on the first floor.'

It took Henry a few moments to grasp the significance of this news.

'Full,' he enquired. 'Full.' Henry was stunned. 'Full,' he repeated for the third time. 'We have to wait for one of them to book out?'

'Well I haven't heard it expressed quite like that before,' replied Mrs Lloyd-King. 'It's usually a bit more biblical, but I think you've grasped the system. When one of our residents dies a room becomes available for a new resident. However as no one on the dementia floor is on a life support machine at this precise moment in time, it's unlikely to be imminent.'

Henry felt the blood drain from his face. 'I hadn't realised.' He paused. 'I suppose it's obvious really.'

Back in the car Audrey spoke at last.

'She could be with us for months; years. Check the insurance on the house,' she added in a resigned voice.

But a solution was forming in Henry's mind. It was unthinkable, unspeakable, and he quickly dismissed it. However, when one month became two and two became three, with no updates from Morderton Manor, the 'solution' came back and began to take hold. After all, they were all expected to die. It wouldn't come as a shock when one of them did. Given the financial burden, the family might even see it as a godsend, and maybe, just maybe, Henry might be able to help the Grim Reaper out with this one. He tried to put the appalling idea out of his mind but he could not stop wondering how it might be done. The first floor; that was going to be the problem he mused.

Sylvia had quipped that Morderton Manor was as secure as Colditz and it was undoubtedly true that none of the residents were going to escape even if they wanted to. However, the security system was not designed to stop anyone breaking in.

Who would want to? Henry's crazy plan to circumvent the waiting list was off the radar. It had to be possible thought Henry.

Morderton Manor overlooked Lincombe Park Golf Course and an initial reccie suggested that the only way to break into the home would be from the golf course, and at night when only a skeleton staff was on duty. A round of golf was quickly booked and Henry proceeded around the course with his golfing equipment supplemented by a pair of binoculars and a rather bulky camera. He had looked in the mirror before leaving and saw a rotund, balding, middle aged man, with a not inconsiderable paunch and spectacles. I wouldn't get a job as a double for Tom Cruise he thought; too tall for a start. He was constantly ribbed about his likeness to Captain Mainwaring of Dad's Army fame by those old enough to remember the television programme, or who still enjoyed the endless repeats. He reasoned that it could be worse. What would it be like if he was a dead ringer for James Corden or Johnny Vegas? At least the percentage of the population who felt compelled to stare gormlessly at him was inevitably decreasing with time. It was unfortunate that by the time they had all shaken off their mortal coils he'd have taken up residence in some graveyard himself. As he stared at his reflection in the mirror he pondered again on the fact that it wasn't the actor Arthur Lowe who stared back at him, rather a brother who closely resembled him. He returned to the task at hand, confident that breaking into Morderton Manor wasn't going to be beyond his ingenuity. A few days later he was less sure. His reconnaissance from the golf course had been surprisingly exhilarating. He had butterflies in his stomach as he surreptitiously inspected Morderton Manor through his binoculars. His hands were shaking as he removed his camera from his golf bag. He had to calm himself before snapping the retirement home from every conceivable angle. As his reconnaissance continued around its perimeter fence, he was morphing into the action hero lying dormant within his unlikely exterior. He had the exhilarating feeling that he was becoming his father's son.

Henry had never known his father. He had a vague recollection of a kindly man telling him to pull himself together; a shadowy snapshot of a distant memory. All his mother had told him was that he was a dodgy character with a criminal past, and, if still alive, was probably incarcerated in a high security jail. Henry knew in his heart of hearts that he was probably an unsavoury character, but he embraced the image of a twenty first century Robin Hood. While other children idolised James Bond, Henry was enthralled by Goldfinger and Dr No. His parental fantasies were an antidote to the fact that his schoolboy experience had not been a happy one. Two disproportionally large front teeth had led to Henry acquiring the unfortunate nickname 'Horsey,' while a fear of snakes to the point of paranoia led to a perverse form of bullying. Putting a pet corn snake on Henry's lap ensured a dramatic reaction whose comic value never seemed to wane. He became a solitary child in whose dreams Horsey Hetherington became an all conquering Blofeld.

As Henry returned home from his reconnaissance he knew that he was living his dream. The dream soon turned to reality when Henry studied his photographs. Any commander could have told him that the devil is in the detail. The plan was relatively simple and there didn't seem to be an alternative. The doors were locked so entry would have to be through a window. The ground floor windows were alarmed, ostensibly to stop intruders, but really to discourage any attempt to abscond for an evening by the compos mentis inmates on the ground floor. That left entering through a first floor window. He would need wire cutters to enter the grounds, a ladder, and tools with which to access the window. Currently he possessed an old wooden ladder and a small box of tools from B & Q. What was he to do?

A pragmatic man he opted to attempt a trial run to properly assess the feasibility of his plan. The following Sunday afternoon, while Audrey was at the p.m. version of a coffee morning, Henry attempted to enter the house through a bedroom window. He retrieved his ladder from the back of the garage and immediately noticed how heavy it was. Carrying it through the golf course wasn't going to be a walk in the park. He carefully placed it under the window. Although only on the first floor it felt a remarkably long way up as he proceeded to climb towards it. The higher he got the more aware he became that no one was holding the bottom. When he finally reached the top of the ladder he couldn't bring himself to let go of it with both hands. He managed to open the window, which he had left slightly ajar, with one hand, and after several anxious minutes he summoned up the courage to continue and pulled himself through it. He got up from the bedroom floor and immediately discarded any idea of now leaving the house by the same method.

A dejected Henry realised that he would have to come up with a method of entering Morderton Manor at night which didn't involve the skills of a cat burglar. Brains rather than brawn were required and Henry was feeling positive again as he racked his brains for a solution. He spent time in the library perusing the plots of the novels in the crime fiction section, good and not so good, in search of inspiration, but all to no avail. As a debilitating sense of desperation set in, Morderton Manor remained impregnable. Henry resigned himself to an eternity of bickering from an increasingly irate and hostile wife. Mother had meanwhile rediscovered a youthful passion for naturism which was causing Audrey endless embarrassment. A tactless remark by Henry about the reduction in laundry, intended to lighten the atmosphere, served only to enrage her further. His only consolation was that eventually nature would take its course, and remove one of the inmates on the first floor.

In this darkest hour hope was to come from an unexpected source. Ruth Hollingsworth was going to Canada for three weeks and had asked Audrey if she would visit her mother, a resident of Morderton Manor, while the family were abroad. Audrey had promised to visit her each week. Henry wasn't sure at this point how he was going to convert this opportunity to his advantage, but he did know that it would probably be his only opportunity. He evaluated the possibilities that this turn of events offered. Once again, Henry had a plan.

'Mrs Dowling. You want to come with me?' Audrey asked in amazement. 'Why?'

Chapter Three

On Thursday the twenty-seventh, Henry was waiting for his wife in the car park of Morderton Manor when she arrived from work. She seemed surprised to see him, as though she hadn't really believed that he'd be there.

Mrs Dowling was a tall thin woman who had obviously been eagerly awaiting their arrival. She beamed when they entered the room and within a few minutes they were being transported to life in Kenya after the war.

'Daddy had a plantation up country,' she informed them in a cut glass voice.

Henry and Audrey quickly discovered that they were not expected to contribute to the conversation. Henry stayed for about ten minutes before he made his excuses and left, leaving Audrey to reminiscences of marauding elephants, unreliable servants, sumptuous colonial balls, and government officials who apparently lacked any.

He strode purposefully to the lift, entered 132, and headed up to the first floor. He had his story prepared if he was spotted. 'I just wanted to see mother's floor again'. Keep it simple. The lift door opened and he stepped out into an empty corridor. The gods were smiling on him. No time to hesitate. He went straight to a bedroom and opened the door. It was obviously a woman's room and it was empty. He took a deep breath and stepped inside. As he walked towards the bed, Sophie Delouche was in the dining room eating her beef bourguignon. Ironically there were thirteen seated around the table, because this was to be her last supper. As Henry slid under the bed he realised that this would be his first actual criminal act and he had no certainty as to the consequences which would follow.

It seemed an eternity before she finally entered the room, and she was accompanied by a member of staff who seemed in no hurry as she helped her to get ready for bed, and then tucked her in for the night. Henry waited for about ten minutes after she had left before girding his loins for the task ahead and creating an unexpected vacancy at Morderton Manor.

After regaining his composure, he took one last look at the lifeless body of Sophie Delouche staring at the ceiling. Her eyes still had a strangely startled expression. He closed her eyelids and she suddenly appeared quite serene. He was surprised by his own lack of emotion. He felt no sadness, but of course he hadn't known her. They were two ships that collided in the night. He felt no guilt, no remorse; only pride in his own professionalism and satisfaction in a job well done. It was with confidence that he headed to the lift. He walked purposefully to the reception area which was empty apart from a middle aged woman behind the desk who was typing on a laptop and barely acknowledged him. He hadn't signed the visitors register when he arrived. There was no point in advertising the fact that he was present at a murder scene just in case it hadn't gone to plan, but he feigned signing out before calmly leaving the building and heading for his car. As he drove off he felt a wave of optimism flow over him. He had committed the perfect murder and his only regret was that he was the only person who would ever know. Realising that there was always the possibility, however remote, of an overzealous coroner suspecting foul play, Henry lay low and waited patiently for the telephone call from Mrs Lloyd-King. However, after a week had passed he was becoming disillusioned with the obvious inefficiency of Morderton Manor which was at odds with its imposing facade. He threw caution to the wind and phoned to enquire if there was any movement in the vacancy situation on the first floor. The receptionist had a more corporate telephone manner than the young girl they had met on their first visit. She made it clear, politely but firmly, that prospective guests were not expected to have such enquires made on their behalf.

'Hearse chasing is frowned upon,' she explained. 'You will be notified as soon as a room becomes available.'

As Henry knew that a room was available he became increasingly frustrated with their conversation and was eventually put through to Mrs Lloyd-King. That conversation

17

was to turn his frustration into incredulity, closely followed by a gut retching despair.

'Waiting list? What waiting list? No one mentioned a waiting list.'

Mrs Lloyd-King was not conciliatory by nature. She was used to standing her ground, and she considered Henry Hetherington-Busby a comparative lightweight anyway.

'I can assure you that you would have been told you were on a waiting list. Everyone is and we would have no reason to make you an exception.' She spoke slowly and with emphasis. Henry was left in no doubt that the matter was not going to be debated.

'Good God, we're no further forward,' muttered Henry.

'Your mother has been on our waiting list for less than four months,' replied Mrs Lloyd-King in exasperation. 'Edward Whitelaw's mother-in-law has been waiting for over a year. Elizabeth Arnold has been on the list for almost eight months. You have only two people ahead of you on the first floor waiting list,' she continued, 'and in the past we have had occasions when it has been in double figures.'

Henry offered no comment. She tried to lighten the mood with the only piece of good news she possessed. One of our elderly gentlemen on the first floor has taken a turn for the worse,' she confided. 'We're probably talking weeks, not months. So the system does work, if somewhat slowly.'

Totally deflated, Henry thanked her for her time and put down the phone.

This was a severe setback. Audrey had one more visit with Mrs Dowling, and three more residents on the first floor had to meet their maker before mother could claim her place in Morderton Manor.

Henry put the accounts of The Dog and Duck public house to one side. He reminded himself that this was probably going to be his last window of opportunity, and that fortune favoured the brave. He considered the problem rationally and logically. Three residents of the first floor had to meet their maker. If they all passed away on the same night, suspicions would undoubtedly be aroused. Even if MRSA or salmonella was the original suspect, the ensuing investigations could lead anywhere including to his door.

Yet fate had intervened in the crisis. God was now sorting one out through natural causes and leaving Henry with only two to deal with. This presented a very different scenario. The residents were all awaiting a visit from the Grim Reaper; maybe not imminently, but sooner rather than later. Two in one night would surely be accepted as bad luck. Or good luck thought Henry. It depended on your point of view. His confidence was rising.

He considered his plan of action. Realistically, the first phase and victim one should present no problems. He'd have to make sure it was a woman but the room decor should make this quite apparent. With his present run of luck, he had to make sure he wasn't despatching the resident already earmarked for the afterlife. It would be a carbon copy of his first foray into mercy killing. Mercy killing with a twist, he mused, with Mother being the recipient of the compassion. Phase two, victim two, on the same night. That would be trickier. However, he could stay in number one's bedroom until number two would be asleep, and he had noticed that the rooms all contained a comfortable fire side chair. It was, on reflection, very straight forward. A very achievable plan thought Henry, and he had every confidence that he would achieve it. He returned to the accounts of The Dog and Duck.

Over supper he asked Audrey when she was visiting Mrs Dowling again.

'Tomorrow night.'

'Good. I'm coming with you again.'

Audrey said nothing. He'd been acting very strangely recently.

When Audrey drove into the Morderton Manor car park the following evening Henry was sitting patiently on a step awaiting her arrival. Once again Henry only entered Audrey's name in the visitor's book. He wanted no connection to Morderton Manor. There was going to be a double murder tonight.

Mrs Dowling was again eagerly awaiting their visit, determined to entertain them with more fascinating reminiscences of life in the African bush. After ten minutes Henry made his excuses without embarrassment and took the lift up to the first floor. Once again the corridor was deserted, and he slid under the bed in what was obviously a very feminine woman's room. The hard floor was giving him rapidly deteriorating backache but eventually the door opened and the woman entered. He heard the carer calmly tell her, step by step, how to get ready for bed. Ground Hog day was obviously a common by-product of increasing life expectancy. The carer gave her some medication and left her tucked up in bed. Henry decided to give her time to fall asleep before despatching her to the hereafter. It was at this point that things started to go off plan. He heard the door open and somebody walked quietly but resolutely to the bed. He saw the mattress sink towards him as an obviously heavy person lay on top of her. He felt her legs move but not with the vigour of Sophie Delouche. He heard her groans although they were not the shrieks of Sophie Delouche. The drugs thought Henry. It had to be down to the medication. He realised that he was witnessing, in so far as one could tell from under a bed, a copycat murder. Someone in the home had deduced how Sophie Delouche had died and had decided to replicate it. Imitation may be the highest form of flattery but Henry was not amused. This might aid him tonight but would the assailant above him know when to stop. This could be a one off execution. On the other hand the assailant above him could be a homicidal maniac who wouldn't want to stop. Then Henry heard a last convulsive shudder followed by silence. He felt the assailant get off the bed after a few minutes and leave the room as quietly as he had entered it.

Henry slid from under the bed and stood up. He looked at the woman below him. She was obviously tired from her exertions but very much alive and looked at him with the perplexity of someone to whom total incomprehension was the norm. Henry sighed. He lay on top of her and picked up the pillow.

He had been sitting in the fireside chair, mentally preparing for phase two, when he heard the door handle turn. He immediately reacted and hid behind the side of the wardrobe. A man in a dressing gown walked quickly into the room and towards the bed. He looked at the floor and gave an audible sigh of relief as he picked up what appeared to be a pair of underpants. As he turned he faced Henry who was standing alongside the wardrobe. The men stared at each other for what could only have been a few moments, but which seemed an eternity. Neither spoke. The man turned and walked quickly out of the door. Henry broke into a sweat. This was definitely not in the plan. Phase two was mentally aborted as he descended into a blind panic. He was struggling to come to terms the situation that he suddenly found himself in. He was standing in a room with a dead woman who had possibly been raped before he had killed her, and a witness to his being there was wandering through the corridors at this precise moment. He had to get out of the building. He opened the door and walked swiftly to the lift. Once on the ground floor he checked that the corridor was clear and headed briskly across the hall. Reception was empty and he ran straight to the door. This was when he discovered that the door was locked.

Sitting in reception in the dark, Henry considered his position. His optimism had evaporated and his mood was dark. Who was the secret lover? Was the sex consensual? Was she drugged? Would she have remembered anything in the morning if he hadn't killed her? How in God's name was he going to get out of here?

Audrey was tired. The only drug Mrs Dowling appeared to be on was caffeine. It was nine o'clock when an uncompromising carer informed her that, regardless of her protestations, visiting time was over and her guest would have to leave. Audrey breathed a sigh of relief, kissed her goodnight, and drove home, only to discover that there was no sign of Henry. She felt exhausted, and retired to bed. He could sort out his own supper. Her head hit the pillow and she fell asleep.

When she woke up the bedroom was in total darkness due to the blackout curtains, but she knew that something was wrong. In her drowsy state she struggled to determine what it was. She couldn't hear anything. That was it. She couldn't hear Henry breathing. What was the time? She put on the bedside light and looked at the clock. It was twenty past three. He must have fallen asleep downstairs. She got up and made her way downstairs but there was no sign of Henry. She pulled open the curtain and looked outside. The car wasn't there. She sat down in the lounge and did nothing for ten minutes. She got up and rang his mobile but it was switched off. He never switched his mobile off. She felt uneasy and not a little concerned. Was Henry in some sort of trouble and, if so, how serious was it?

Could he be having an affair?

It seemed highly implausible and she quickly dismissed the idea from her mind. Around four fifteen tiredness got the better of her and she found herself becoming increasingly drowsy. She went back to bed and quickly fell into a deep sleep.

Dawn broke over Morderton Manor, the doors were unlocked, and people started to arrive. Henry, who had been awake all night, was now in a position to vacate the building, but the receptionist had been one of the first to arrive, and there always appeared to be someone sitting on one of the settees. Then there was a flurry of activity, hushed whispers, and a string of telephone calls. The body had been discovered. Henry was lying behind one of the settees and only some divine intervention would allow him to leave unnoticed. His sense of panic was only compounded by the distant sound of a hoover moving slowly but relentlessly towards him.

Chapter Four

Henry was not the only occupant who had not slept as dawn broke over Morderton Manor. James Berkley OBE was confused and not a little concerned by the turn of events earlier that evening. Widowed at a relatively early age, James had quickly discovered that there was a large pool of unattached widows in his home town of Winkford to whom he appeared to present a particularly good catch. He was of medium height, fit, healthy, in possession of his own teeth and hair, and, most importantly in the final analysis, financially secure and still breathing. Far from being lonely as old age approached, he found himself enjoying the company of a string of elderly but well maintained cougars from the blue rinse brigade. James was enjoying his retirement. He looked forward to the weekend visits from his children and grandchildren, who remained oblivious to granddad's amorous activities during the week, and he saw this idyllic lifestyle perpetuating into the foreseeable future.

Fate intervened, and dealt a cruel blow. He became the latest victim in a string of burglaries targeting senior citizens. The victims were mainly residents of Surrey although the gang occasionally crossed into the adjoining counties of Hampshire, Berkshire, and Middlesex. However, a disproportionate number of the burglaries had been in Woking and Winkford and the police were convinced that the criminals involved lived in that area, a fact widely reported in the local press. His family showed an unwelcome concern. Press sensationalism of what was described as an epidemic of crime against the elderly heightened their concern. A local newspaper report on the attempted robbery of the exorbitantly expensive jewellery of Dame Hayley Shirsom, who was out of the country at the time, was the final straw. Thwarted in their attempts to locate them the gang had ripped up all the soft furnishings. It was not clear if this was in spiteful frustration or in an attempt to find their hiding place. The hiding place turned out to be a safety deposit box in the local branch of Barclays, but their efforts led them to be christened 'The Ripper Gang' by the Winkford Chronicle. It was a title quickly adopted by the rest of the media and played some part in determining James Berkley's future. His protestations fell on deaf ears and, despite being a retired director of a quoted company, he found himself being bundled off to Morderton Manor for his own protection.

He quickly settled into the comfortable life there. The building and the grounds were impressive, the food was of restaurant standard, the staff courteous and attentive, and his new found companions were mostly of an easy going disposition. However the building was totally devoid of cougars and, while he was in no way a prisoner, it was totally unsuitable for that kind of entertaining. James Berkley felt that his life was incomplete.

That changed when Shirley Simpson took up residence in the dementia floor upstairs. James, who had known her since childhood, took it upon himself to visit her, although he had always considered her to be dull and uninspiring. However it was while visiting her that he had met the lovely Linda Grisham who was elegance and charm personified. It was unfortunate that she didn't retain any memory of him from one visit to another, but in La La Land she was a gem in a beach of pebbles.

The initial nocturnal encounter had been an anxious and worrying affair, but that now seemed a lifetime ago. While Linda had obviously no idea who he was when he entered her room, always seemed startled as he entered her bed, and was uncomprehendingly vacant throughout the act, she was always acquiescent and compliant. Thus James felt assured that the sex was consensual, at least in a legal sense. These night time trysts had become as routine as his afternoon strolls, and he was serenely happy with the direction in which his life was heading. However it now appeared that he had a rival. Who was the strange man in her bedroom? The more he thought about it the more perplexed he became. He didn't recognise him, so presumably he was a first floor resident. Were they capable of such an act? Had he maybe just randomly wandered into her room? But why was he fully dressed in a lounge suit in the middle of the night? It defied any logical explanation.

During breakfast there was a bustle of activity amongst the staff and it was evident that something was afoot. By ten o'clock the news of a death on the first floor was common knowledge in every part of Morderton Manor except, of course, the first floor. That was when he started to worry; really worry.

When Audrey woke up it was ten past ten and there was still no sign of Henry. Unease became fear and she ran to the window and pulled open the curtains. She looked out of the window and the car was back in the driveway. The feeling of relief was palpable and she put on her dressing gown and went downstairs.

Henry was sat at the kitchen table staring at his coffee. Exhausted and deflated, the possible consequences of his actions were becoming apparent to him. He could just as easily be sitting in a police interview room as at his kitchen table. As the hoover had entered the reception area he had run out of options. He simply stood up and turned to the bookcase behind the sofa. He could feel accusing eyes boring into him as he stared at the books for a few moments. Yet, when he turned round there were no eyes on him. There must have been half a dozen people scattered around reception, not to mention the receptionist, but all were engrossed in their reading or their conversations. No one noticed Henry as he rose from behind the settee, pale and exhausted. They paid scant attention to him as he walked to the visitors register, feigned signing out, and left the building. He walked down the hill to where his car was parked unobtrusively in a small side road. He didn't start shaking until he was sitting in the driver's seat, but when it took hold, it seemed an eternity before it stopped, and he was left with only an uncharacteristic desire to burst into tears to contend with.

Once home, Henry headed straight for the kitchen, made a cup of coffee, and pondered the events of the previous evening. He was acutely aware that he was no longer in control of events, but how precarious was his situation in reality? There was a witness to his being at the scene of the crime, but Henry was a total stranger to him. They had seen each other in the middle of the night by the light from a bedside lamp. Furthermore the witness was guilty of some crime himself. Henry wasn't exactly sure what the gravity of the crime was, but he was sure that the stranger's liaison in the bedroom involved some form of illegality. It was unlikely that he would volunteer any information on the events of the previous evening willingly. If he was removed from the equation, there was no reason to suppose that the dead woman would not be diagnosed as having died in her sleep as initially planned. On the other hand, the second intended victim had gained more than a reprieve as Henry could think of no circumstance in which he would be entering Morderton Manor again. The mysterious stranger had no idea who he was and Henry intended to keep it that way. Failure could lead to a lengthy prison sentence, a prospect which terrified him although he had barely considered it until now. He realised that he would be living with an increasingly unhinged mother and an increasingly desperate wife for an indeterminable period of time. He was struggling to regain his composure when Audrey entered the room. As he looked up the desire to burst into tears washed over him again. Audrey was acutely aware that he appeared to be on the verge of some sort of breakdown.

'Where have you been? What's the matter?'

His distress was so apparent that it brought him the breathing space he required, and after what seemed an interminable period of time, but was actually less than a minute, he came up with a reasonably convincing reply.

'I worry about Mother. It all got on top of me. I needed some space away from here so I took a drive and just sat in a lay-by. I fell asleep.'

Audrey was visibly shocked and upset. She gave him a big hug and told him that he'd got the Mother problem out of all proportion before heading upstairs again to get changed.

Henry considered his evening. It hadn't gone to plan, it certainly hadn't gone well, but it hadn't been the catastrophe that it could so easily have been. He'd had a lucky escape and had no intention of tempting providence. He would lie low and keep well away from Morderton Manor. Utterly exhausted, he finished his third cup of coffee and headed for the office. He sat at his desk and went through the motions without actually doing very much, but he arrived home that evening exhausted and mentally drained. It was Friday, fish night, and one of his favourites, but he apologised to an understanding Audrey, had a quick shower, and went to bed.

He fell asleep almost immediately but he slept fitfully and the dream came back to haunt him for the first time in years.

The little boy was still excited by his birthday party. He couldn't sleep and the laughter from the lounge was beckoning him like a magnet. He made his way downstairs to where he could see the T.V. through the open door. A bit actor was experiencing 'The Curse of the White Serpent' by having his throat ripped out by the giant cobra in the starring role. In horror he watched it hissing with primeval malevolence before lunging towards the camera, fangs fully extended. As he screamed in terror, he heard his father's voice, 'pull yourself together little man; pull yourself together.'

Henry woke with a violent spasm. He knocked over the glass of water on his bedside table as he groped in the dark for the light. Wiping the sweat from his brow he stared at the ceiling.

Audrey stirred beside him. 'I'll make you a cup of tea', she said softly.

Chapter Five

It was two days later that Mrs Lloyd-King received a visit from the local constabulary. The receptionist had initially offered to make an appointment, an offer they had politely declined. As they waited in reception, Mrs Lloyd-King could only assume with some annoyance that the neighbourhood watch issue had once again hit the Surrey County Council agenda. They had an inflated perception of their own importance and didn't seem able to grasp the fact that nobody broke into retirement homes. Apart from being obvious to anyone with half a brain, it was a statistically proven fact. She reflected on how much easier her job would be without the incessant PR involved.

After polite introductions they moved to her office and DI Jones got straight to the point of their visit. The death of Mrs Grisham was not as straightforward as had at first appeared, and was now being investigated as suspicious. Was she aware that Mrs Grisham had had sexual intercourse shortly before she died?

Mrs Lloyd-King experienced an unrecognisable emotion and was initially at a loss for words.

'Sexual intercourse,' she said with distaste. She made it sound like a tropical disease.

'It is becoming increasingly likely that Mrs Grisham was the recipient of foul play,' continued DS Jones. 'However, the presence of DNA should make our apprehension of the culprit relatively straightforward.' Mrs Lloyd listened in horror as DS Jones explained that they would need to take a DNA sample from all the male members of staff.

'To eliminate them from our enquiries,' he added helpfully. However it was when they were all eliminated from their enquiries that Mrs Lloyd-King encountered the full unbridled experience of unrelenting stress.

'You can't take DNA samples from our paying residents,' she exclaimed in horror. 'They pay a fortune to stay here. They don't expect to be treated as criminals.'

'I think you'll find that there's very little we can't do,' replied Jones, 'and that one of them is our criminal.' Mrs Lloyd- King looked shattered, but so it proved to be.

Two days later James Berkley OBE was arrested on suspicion of being implicated in the rape and murder of Mrs Linda Grisham of Morderton Manor, a charge he strenuously denied in the face of overwhelming evidence.

It was DI Jones who, with PC Winch, a bubbly young trainee who had been told to listen and learn, interviewed James Berkley in Guildford Central Police Station. He had been read the mandatory script explaining his rights, and he looked nervous and ill at ease as he sat beside his brief. Yet as the interview proceeded Jones began to have niggling doubts about the extent of his guilt although the evidence to the contrary appeared overwhelming. His defence on the charge of rape appeared to be based on his contention that 'she enjoyed it.' This could at best be described as a technical defence which DS Jones assured him had little chance of standing up in court. James Berkley, however, was convinced that his argument was supported by corroborating evidence. It wasn't as though he'd deflowered her. She was a twice married seventy-six year old, and they'd been doing it for months. DS Jones explained that this line of argument was not supported by any case law he knew of, and reiterated that it had no possibility of standing up in court, but James Berkley appeared to be comfortable with the validity of his defence. He found questions on the mental capacity of Linda Grisham more difficult to deal with, and could only reiterate that as far as he was concerned she had enjoyed the experience every bit as much as he did.

'Did she look forward to the next sexual encounter?'

He was unable to give any answer, satisfactory or otherwise, to that question. However on the charge of murder he was vociferous in his denial. Not only was he innocent, he was a witness to the culprit, a balding, bespectacled, and overweight man, who resembled Captain Mainwaring from Dad's Army and who had disappeared without trace immediately afterwards. Given the evidence of the DNA, his presence at the crime scene was beyond doubt. It followed that his guilt on the charge of murder was also beyond doubt.

Jones was an old hand at such interviews and was both shrewd and perceptive. He was so obviously guilty, and yet his persistent denial of murder had a ring of truth about it. He ignored his brief's advice to remain silent and seemed more annoyed than concerned as he told his most implausible of stories with an assurance that Jones found troubling. After years of listening to the fabrications of the criminal classes, he was never surprised when it was revealed that a celebrated and accomplished actor had done time in the past. He was not easily duped, but if James Berkley was acting he deserved an Oscar for his performance. He never wavered from his story. He never shied away from the detail. He ignored his brief's advice to say nothing, and he never tripped himself up. If only his story wasn't so preposterous. Yet it was. But the doubt could not be dispelled.

Henry reverted to his usual daily routine while showing little outward interest in the story that was enthralling the rest of Surrey and was now national news. The county's historically low crime rate had already appeared to be surging out of control with a spate of headline gabbing burglaries by the Ripper Gang, but now they were being overshadowed by the melodramatic reporting of the Linda Grisham murder in the tabloids. Henry followed the press releases avidly and the reporting of the murder, closely followed by the arrest of James Berkley, quickly lifted his spirits.

The fact that a murder at Morderton Manor was now national news was in no small measure due to the drive and ambition of a young journalist at the Surrey Echo.

At the tender age of twenty-six Zoe Porter was the crime reporter at the Echo. She was also the Local Events reporter, presided over the problem page when the local agony aunt was on holiday, and had even written the horoscopes during the flu epidemic of the previous winter when the paper had struggled on valiantly with a skeleton staff. Her only disaster in four years with the paper had been her one and only attempt to write the gardening column. It transpired that her only experience of gardening had been mowing the lawn. The only positive feedback to come out of the ensuing postbag of complaints was the realisation of just how popular the column was. Zoe was considered a safe pair of hands and the editorial staff were comfortable with a bit of journalistic licence if it sold newspapers. Zoe had concluded at a very early stage in the investigation that this story could be the one which would facilitate her breakthrough into the big time, otherwise known as the tabloids, and that unfettered sensationalism would be the key to opening that door. Morderton Manor became Murderton Manor and the name had become common usage among local people. It had even been adopted by parts of the national press. It was she who had described its forbidding facade, eerie in the moonlight, where the old and frail were sent to die. While the description could be argued, it was at odds with the glossy advertisement they carried for the home on page five of every weekend issue. As for the ghosts haunting its corridors at night; the source of that anecdote was thought by many to be Zoe's fertile imagination. The final straw for the chairman of Knightley Retirement Homes came when she named the assailant as the Murderton Monster, and it was adopted by a couple of tabloids. The management of Knightley Plc. watched in horror as the press coverage of their flagship home adversely affected the entire business. They informed the Echo's management that they were considering legal action and, more worrying; they would exclude it from their advertising budget unless the tone of their articles changed significantly. Zoe was instructed in no uncertain terms to 'tone it down'.

DI Jones was summoned to Chief Superintendent Donovan's office. He knocked and entered with some trepidation as the summons was unusual and his presence was required immediately. C.S. Donovan pointed to a chair and, dispensing with any pleasantries, got straight to the point.

'How's the Pillow Case coming along,' he enquired, for this was the nickname by which the case had become known in the building.

'We have a suspect and we're just tidying up some loose ends,' replied Jones.

'Loose ends.'

John Donovan made the words seem unduly dramatic.

'I'm having a problem with those loose ends of yours. Sir Charles Grisham has been informed that his mother's death is suspicious, and he is a very good friend of the Chief Constable's wife. Both are active members of the local Conservative Party it would appear, and are trustees of several local charities. Chief Constable Stanley Bryant, apparently at the request of his wife, has given Grisham my mobile phone number. Totally unprofessional of course, but I don't expect he considered the consequences. Sir Charles Grisham, who is one of the most boring men on the planet and also appears to have a lot of time on his hands, feels that this gives him the right to cut out the middle men and come straight to me for updates on the case. Several times a day I might add, and I'm running out of convincing crises to get him off the phone. He must be under the impression by now that leafy Surrey is a microcosm of downtown New York. It is becoming particularly tedious because I know that we are holding the suspect, dare I say perpetrator of the crime, in one of our cells. I have a simple question Jones. Why has he not been charged? Do we have some problem of which I have not been made aware? Why am I still getting those phone calls Jones?'

'I've got an uneasy feeling about this one sir,' Jones replied. He was unprepared for this line of questioning.

'You've got an uneasy feeling; an uneasy feeling. That's the lamest excuse for not tying up a watertight case I've ever heard. You've been watching too much Inspector Morse, Jones. We've got a string of burglaries to clear up and you're uneasy about an open and shut case.'

Jones looked embarrassed but unconvinced. C.S. Donovan made a conscious effort to remain calm and summed up the progress in the case to date.

'Let's look at the facts. Our suspect is definitely guilty of rape. We have irrefutable evidence in the form of DNA, so it comes as no surprise that he has put his hand up to that one. The fact that she didn't scream the house down is in his view indicative of consent. The fact that she would have agreed to be fired from a cannon if asked makes a defence based on consent ridiculous. Of course if she had screamed out, that might explain why he put a pillow over her face. Let us now consider the alternative explanation. After raping her, he leaves the room minus his underpants. A ghostly apparition who apparently bears a remarkable similarity to a character in Dad's Army, dressed for a day at the office or a job interview, suddenly appears in the room and suffocates her for no apparent reason. He then hangs around until Berkley returns and collects the aforementioned underpants; obviously a particularly tidy ghoul this one; before mysteriously disappearing again from the securely locked building. It isn't Inspector Morse you need on this case Jones. I suggest you get hold of Jonathon Creek. I believe his first calling is as a stand-up comedian and I'm beginning to think you've both got that in common. Fortunately we have a witness to this ghostly fiend. Once again, it comes as no surprise to find that it's none other than our suspect. So we'll just pop down to the graveyard tonight and put together a line up for Mr Berkley. We wouldn't want his brief to claim we hadn't followed up every line of enquiry, would we Jones? I'm getting pressure over our burglary targets Jones. My mobile phone has been hijacked and I want it back. So I want you to stop your psychic investigations in the nursing home and start some police investigations into the latest Ripper break-ins. Charge Berkley. Visit Grisham and give him any answers or information he requires. Explain the process from now until conviction in as much detail as is possible, and then give him your card. Give him two.'

A couple of hours later Jones read James Berkley his rights and formally charged him with the rape and murder of Linda Grisham. DC Jones put any last lingering doubts that still troubled him out of his mind and quickly wrote up a thorough, if concise, report on the Pillow case; a report which would satisfy any prosecuting barrister and placate the Chief Superintendent. Shortly after that a police car was heading to the home of Sir Charles Grisham with DI Jones and Sergeant Harris. He lived on George Abbot Hill, the most prestigious address in Winkford. The houses were imposing and as secure as modern technology could make them. A short conversation via the intercom and the gate duly opened and they drove inside. A brisk and efficient young woman ushered them in to the study. Sir Charles, the son of Linda Grisham, rose from his chair to greet them and DI Jones couldn't hide his sharp intake of breath. Sir Charles Grisham bore an uncanny resemblance to Captain Mainwaring.

Chapter Six

DI Jones left George Abbot Hill with very mixed emotions. Without doubt he had failed miserably to fulfil his brief and he was certain that Chief Superintendant Donovan would receive a long and uncomfortable call on his mobile in the very near future. However his conviction that the testimony of James Berkley was not to be lightly dismissed had been unequivocally confirmed. DI Jones was a man on a mission.

He was dropped off at his home, a small flat near the centre of Woking, at about 6.30. His long suffering girlfriend, Joyce Morgan, was cooking an evening meal. When he joked that he may be moving to the traffic division in the near future, a bit monotonous but it came with a company car, she had thought for a moment that he might be actually moving to a normal job. It was his way of hiding his real apprehension at the thought of his debriefing in the morning. Detective Superintendent Donovan was not going to be a happy man.

In that at least his instinct was to be proved correct. Chief Superintendent Donovan's mood was sombre. Firstly there was the contention by Jones that the Spectre at the scene of the crime, the ghostly alibi who had mysteriously appeared from thin air and just as mysteriously disappeared again, was none other than Sir Charles Grisham, millionaire son of the dead woman. C.S. Donovan pointed out that his barber was decidedly on the plump side, balding, and wore glasses .Was he to be regarded as a suspect as well?

Jones was not to be dissuaded. 'He doesn't have an alibi.' C.S. Donovan couldn't believe what he was hearing.

'What do you mean he doesn't have an alibi? How do you know he doesn't have an alibi?'

'I asked him,' Jones replied, 'and furthermore he threatened me.'

C.S. Donovan turned off his mobile while DI Jones recounted the details of the interview. 'He used his association with the Chief Constable to threaten me. He said that if I pursued this line of questioning Chief Constable Bryant would be very upset. When I said I didn't respond well to threats, he said it wasn't a threat, just a fact. He repeated that my line of enquiry would make the Chief Constable a very unhappy man.'

C.S. Donovan took a deep intake of breath. 'He's probably just a little upset that he's being asked to prove that he didn't murder his mother. He's probably even more upset that his mystical powers which allow him to fly through solid brick walls, powers which I might add have remained secret for over fifty years, are now common knowledge.'

D.I. Jones remained unimpressed. While his method of entry and departure might remain unexplained, he fitted the description and he didn't have an alibi. In any other case they'd be breaking open the bubbly. Why not in this case?

John Donovan knew he had a point which would be difficult to refute in the future, and he had obviously got the bit between his teeth. He told him to do nothing while he considered how they ought to proceed.

If DI Jones left his interview with Sir Charles Grisham with a conviction that he was in some way linked to his mother's murder, Sir Charles was left with a melancholy premonition of where the enquires into his mother's death may lead, and you could never totally lose a murky past. He reflected on his Achilles heel, as he had done many times in the past; but then its threat had not appeared imminent.

The trouble was he couldn't provide an alibi for the night in question. Indeed there were several other nights where this would also apply. If he became a suspect in the police enquiry, it was entirely probable that his deeply buried past would rise up and destroy his hard earned reputation.

That afternoon John Donovan received a call from the coroner's office. It appeared that an elderly woman with dementia had died in Morderton Manor only a few weeks earlier, and the circumstances now appeared suspicious. A new post-mortem had been requested and foul play was anticipated. James Berkley OBE was in danger of becoming a celebrity for all the wrong reasons. He concluded that a phone call to the Chief Constable would be prudent at this point. While the

36

widening case against James Berkley was the main topic of conversation, he was careful to bring the loose ends around Sir Charles Grisham's testimony to his attention. John Donovan had been around long enough to sense when minding ones back was judicious.

As the conversation ended, Chief Constable Stanley Bryant was also feeling some anxiety. His wife's friendship with Sir Charles Grisham was escalating from annoying to concerning. The spate of unsolved burglaries by what the media had christened the Ripper Gang was putting him under immense pressure. The last thing he needed was even the hint of a personal connection to a suspect in a murder enquiry, especially one which was turning into a media circus. To his wife, Sarah, Sir Charles Grisham's social circle represented the Winkford elite, and she aspired to be part of it. Stanley had no such pretentions and he tolerated them politely, but when she gave Chief Superintendent Donovan's private work number to Grisham, she had abused her position and compromised his. The fact that Grisham was proving to be a constant irritation, phoning John Donovan every day to get updates on the ensuing inquiries, only exacerbated the problem. After the resulting domestic, Sarah was left stunned and shaken. Stanley Bryant had breathed a sigh of relief, confident that this was an error of judgement which wouldn't be repeated.

It was while he was in this sunny frame of mind that he picked up C.S. Donovan's phone call.

'Serial Killer; doesn't have an alibi?' He felt a deepening sense of foreboding about the Grisham connection.

Zoe Porter got a phone call from her source in Morderton Manor as she was about to leave the office. She remained at her desk and worked late to ensure that news of a second suspicious death in the retirement home filled the front page of the Echo the following day.

Henry was concerned. Could asphyxiation be determined by a post-mortem? Could it be determined by a post-mortem after this length of time? Henry didn't know and he wasn't going to ask anyone, not even Google. As he waited for the result his calm exterior belied his anxiety.

As the press descended on Morderton Manor, Mrs Lloyd-King felt that she was on a roller coaster ride and she had no doubt that the final destination would be her resignation or a mental breakdown unless the investigation into the pillow case was brought to a satisfactory conclusion, and quickly. She was becoming a local celebrity, a development she viewed with horror and distaste. The lurid fascination with her was brought home forcefully when a middle aged woman approached her in Waitrose and asked for her autograph.

While any suspicion that Sir Charles might be involved in the case, other than as Linda Grisham's son, remained the sole conjecture of DI Jones, the possibility of a serial killer in the home now appeared to be a real possibility. In Winkford, indeed the entire county, the results of the imminent autopsy on Sophie Delouche were awaited with morbid and excited anticipation and nowhere more eagerly than at the crime desk of the Echo. The possibility of there being a serial killer at Morderton Manor was now national news and Zoe Porter was becoming noticed in Fleet Street. The last verdict she wanted was death by natural causes. Yet a much greater potential threat was about to be unleashed on Knightley Plc. and Zoe was about to land yet another exclusive which, while not directly connected to the murder, would ultimately lead to her being employed by a local television channel.

Black Dog Productions, a company specialising in budget films which went straight to DVD, was in the early stages of making a film loosely based on the pillow case. This only came to light when they asked if Morderton Manor could be used as a backdrop to some of the action. Zoe Porter had received a phone call from her source that evening, and a little research revealed that their most recent film had been 'Rage of the lesbian vampires'.

Juliet Lloyd-King was instructed by the chairman of Knightley Plc. to accept a request to meet with them and find out what the word 'loosely' meant in cinematic terms. Jack from Black Dog Productions, because she never did get his surname, opened by saying that he felt the film had the potential to put Morderton Manor on the map.

A horrified Juliet Lloyd-King was informed that it would not be completely factual as it had to be entertaining. It was to be an asphyxiation movie based on the murders at Morderton Manor.

'But people aren't paying to see a documentary. They watch Panorama if that's their bag.'

The killer would be part of an ancient Viking cult and the film was going to be called 'Murder Rape and Pillows.' Due to all the victims being in bed there was every opportunity to sex it up a bit, and there would obviously be more victims. Her character was to be played by an up and coming actress called Chelsea Stanford-Love. Her stage name he explained. She was described as a leggy blonde, a bit younger than Mrs Lloyd-King. He didn't specify how much younger. She would play a pivotal part in the plot and would be stalked by the psychotic killer throughout the film. He laughingly informed her that the film would reach its climax just as she did. The psychotic Nordic would fall through a window and end up impaled on a pitchfork.

Juliet Lloyd-King who had remained stunned throughout his monologue finally broke her silence.

'Pitchfork ! Why would there be a pitchfork in the garden?'

Jack laughed 'It's a tried and tested ending at Black Dog Films. It'll make a change from pillows,' he added as an afterthought.

She started to formulate her synopsis to the board of Knightley Homes. It would not make comfortable reading and would include her resignation as a separate appendage.

Three days later the coroner's report landed on Chief Superintendent Donovan's desk. The report started by exonerating the original coroner from any blame which might be apportioned. Death by natural causes was a reasonable assumption in the circumstances. A seventy-eight year old woman dies in her bed in an exclusive nursing home with no visible signs of foul play. Why would a coroner suspect that she might be the victim of a serial killer?

But she was.

The next step was to look at any other similar deaths since James Berkley had entered the home, and there had been several. Morderton Manor could go down in criminal history alongside 10, Rillington Place and Whitechapel.

Henry turned on the television and listened to the local news programme with increasing optimism. It appeared that James Berkley would soon stand accused of both murders although he was yet to be charged with the murder of Sophie Delouche. The police didn't seem to be looking for any other suspects although they were apparently looking for more victims. With the benefit of hindsight, he wished he'd finished off his third intended victim when he had the chance. He started to consider the possibility of bringing the pillow case to a satisfactory conclusion. Initially, the shocking unpredictability of events at his last murderous endeavour, coupled with the fact that a witness to his being at the scene of the crime was residing in the building, had been enough to deter him from even considering any further visits. However, with James Berkley taking up residence at HM Prison, Coldingley, with a seemingly watertight case against him, Henry began to speculate on whether he might pay the retirement home another visit and finish what he had started. On careful consideration he concluded that a third killing would be as reckless as the coroner would be thorough. However, assuming that Berkley got a long stretch for killing two old ladies, this did mean that he would be able to visit Mother as often as he wanted to when she eventually moved in.

When DI Jones and PC Winch walked into the interview room at HM Prison Coldingley, eleven miles from Winkford, James Berkley was already sitting at the table with his brief. Jones read him his rights and then informed him that he was also being charged with the murder of Sophie Delouche almost four months earlier. Furthermore, the deaths of several other women were being looked at again. Jones then began to question him.

When he got back to the station he went straight to C.S. Donovan's office, knocked and entered.

'Innocent. What do you mean innocent?' John Donovan stared at him in disbelief while Jones looked positively smug.

'He has a cast-iron alibi for the evening of the Delouche murder. It will have to be verified, but I have no doubt that it will be. So unless we have two psychos targeting the same retirement home, and using the same methods, he didn't kill the Grisham woman either.'

Chapter Seven

C.S. Donovan could only guess at the press headlines which would greet the British public in the morning. The media hype meant that this murderer was attaining celebrity status. But who was the celebrity? They were no closer to the answer than they were on the day Linda Grisham was discovered dead in her bed.

Two days later James Berkley OBE returned to Morderton Manor in triumph, where Mrs Lloyd–King had arranged the party usually reserved for birthdays which contained a zero. The media were now portraying him as a victim of police incompetence and he was basking in a very different form of celebrity status. No interview was considered inconvenient and a picture of him holding a glass of champagne was on the front page of most newspapers that day. Henry felt increasingly deflated as he watched the television updates and he waited anxiously for the police statement which was expected that afternoon.

At around the same time C.S. John Donovan was having a tense telephone conversation with Chief Constable Stanley Bryant, whom he was bringing up to date with the latest developments in the pillow case, and whose sense of foreboding was deepening as he considered their implications.

'What about the DNA evidence? I thought that was conclusive.'

'It was conclusive proof of rape,' replied Donovan, 'but the Crown Prosecution Service has concluded that it would be difficult to prove, now that he appears to be in the clear on the murder rap. Consent between adults, or the lack of it, is apparently a grey area in the eyes of the CPS, even if one of the participants is completely gaga. I'm afraid they're not going to pursue it and we've had to release him.'

Stanley Bryant felt that the pillow case was now completely out of control and that his wife's friendship with Charles Grisham was becoming increasingly problematic.

'We can hardly charge Charles Grisham on the grounds that he fits the description of some apparition who appeared at the murder scene, and was only witnessed by our last suspect; a suspect who was looking forward to twenty years of Her Majesty's hospitality before he came up with his alibi. Incidentally, the Charles Grisham spectre's most convincing means of entry or escape appears to be transportation from The Star Ship Enterprise.'

C.S. Donovan pointed out that James Berkley was no longer a suspect but their chief witness, their only witness. Grisham fitted his description of the suspect, was the son of the murdered woman, and couldn't provide an alibi for the days of the murders. In the circumstances, however improbable they felt his guilt may be, he had to be taken in for questioning. Furthermore, Donovan admitted candidly, 'he's the only suspect we've got.'

Bryant reluctantly agreed and wondered at what point he should inform his wife. As he put the phone down he wondered if his last promotion was an elevation in rank too far. Was it worth the kudos, prestige, and salary? He seemed far removed from policing as he became increasingly involved in the move from the nineteenth century building which housed the Police Headquarters in Guildford to a new state of the art building in Leatherhead, while also grappling with increasingly unrealistic targets and draconian constraints on overtime. The pressure that a succession of unsolved burglaries over the last year was putting on his limited resources was nothing to the pressure it was putting on him. Meetings with architects and builders for which he was technically ill equipped, difficult targets, impossible deadlines, and uncomfortable conversations with the Home Office, were only exceeded by the demands and expectations of an uppish social climber, his wife Sarah, and she was uncomfortably close to their only suspect.

Stanley Bryant had been fast tracked through the ranks based initially on his possession of a first class degree from Warwick University. The fact that Medieval History had little bearing on day to day police work appeared to be irrelevant to the trendy new broom from the Home Office who had interviewed him. Rising quickly through the ranks to the giddy heights of Chief Constable was testament to his natural ability in the business of crime prevention and detection. He enjoyed police work and revelled in the apprehension and conviction of those on the wrong side of the law.

When he married Sarah Arnold he left his working class roots and joined the upper middle class in one simple ceremony. Pub grub had been upgraded to a la carte, Cotes de Rhone to Pouilley Fuisse, and his mortgage was now as impressive as his house was imposing. He looked back fondly to simpler, more carefree times. His wife, Sarah, beautiful and intelligent, was very much her mother's daughter, and her mother, even in her twilight years, retained those qualities but had gained an easy charm which only comes with maturity. She was however showing the early signs of dementia and they appeared to be advancing more quickly than was the norm. A pragmatic woman, she accepted her fate with fortitude and was determined to manage it as best she could. She would soon be leaving her house on George Abbot Hill and downsizing to life in Morderton Manor. Stanley was determined to ensure that any homicidal maniac residing in that building would be safely behind bars before she moved, but the only leads to date had led them up blind alleys. He had to ensure that the crimes were solved quickly and would use all the resources at his disposal to catch this killer before his mother-in-law entered the retirement home. Stanley was very fond of his mother-in-law and knew that she was equally fond of him. He ranked in her affections alongside Pasha her elderly overweight cat that was as protective towards her as he was spiteful to the rest of the human race. His claws had drawn blood from many a man who had leant forward to give her a gentlemanly peck on the cheek. If it had been a dog it would have been put down years ago. Sarah had agreed to take in her mother's cat when she moved and Stanley assumed it would modify its behaviour when it realised who was feeding it. He would prefer an evening with the cat than in the company of Charles Grisham. If only he could turn out to be a psychopath he thought ruefully.

Later that afternoon C. S. Donovan gave a statement to the press in which he stated that in the light of new evidence James Berkley was no longer a suspect and was being released. Asked if they had any other suspects, he replied that they did have another line of enquiry but he was unable to give them any details as yet. He took no more questions.

As he considered the implications of the police statement Henry could feel his confidence ebbing away. What was this new line of enquiry? James Berkley had been a stroke of luck that would not be repeated. His quick arrest with conclusive D.N.A. evidence had meant that his description of the other man in Linda Grisham's bedroom had never been taken seriously. It would be now. If the police now circulated an accurate description of him, his future prospects were looking much more precarious. Given his inside knowledge he could think of no other line of enquiry. Henry phoned his office and left a message to the effect that he was sick and wouldn't be in work tomorrow. He poured himself a glass of scotch and sank into depression.

Meanwhile, on George Abbot Hill, Charles Grisham was sitting in his study with a bottle of brandy as he reflected on his life; the journey which had taken him to this point where he might imminently be arrested on a charge of murder in the first degree.

He had not been an academic child. Leaving school at the tender age of sixteen he had found employment in the warehouse of a lower end of the market furniture retailer, Carter and Bishop Furniture Ltd, commonly known as C.B.F Ltd, and affectionately known as 'Chip and Board' within the company.

Charlie, as he was known then, was a conscientious and likeable employee and at the relatively young age of twenty-four he was relocated to Reading as an Assistant Manager. He was happy, confident, and competent, and would undoubtedly have remained at C.B.F., steadily climbing its corporate ladder, had his careernot been unceremoniously cut short just eighteen months later.

Peter Spier, Mr Angry of Pangbourne, entered the store on a fateful Saturday when Charles was the duty manager, and he was furious. This would come as no surprise to those who knew him. However, on this occasion, Peter Spier, serial whinger and seasoned complainer, had a legitimate reason to be upset. This was his third visit to C.B.F. Reading to collect the table and chairs which he had been informed were now in stock. Yet again this turned out to be an error. A case of computer says 'yes' when the answer was 'no'. He went to the customer service desk and informed the receptionist that on this occasion he would not be leaving the store without his furniture. The young girl on reception asked him if he'd brought a sleeping bag. Even by C.B.F. customer service standards this was an unhelpful comment .Peter Spier demanded to see the manager. This in itself was not an unusual occurrence and Charlie approached him with confidence. He could be charming, sincere, and calm in the presence of the most difficult of customers, but Peter Spier would not be reasoned with. He became ever more belligerent and it became apparent that he would not leave without his furniture, and his furniture wasn't in the building. The store didn't close for four hours and Charlie had run out of options. He felt himself become very calm as he asked Peter Spier to remain on the shop floor for a moment while he tried to resolve the problem. He walked purposely to the Managers Office and when he returned he had an empty wastepaper basket in his hand. He placed it in front of Peter Spier and said in a slow measured voice,

'Abracadabra.'

He said it three times and then looked up at an incredulous Peter Spier.

'Well that didn't work. Have you got any ideas?'

Peter Spier's naturally ruddy complexion turned scarlet and he was visibly shaking as he caught Charlie by the knot of his tie and pulled him violently towards him. Peter Spier was a large man, but Charlie Grisham, while below average height and on the tubby side, was young and fit. His response was as spontaneous and as it was ill-considered.

What followed had several interpretations. Charlie's barrister described it as an aggressive defence in the face of an unprovoked attack. That interpretation had a limited following.

The police prosecutor described it as aggravated assault. The duty doctor in casualty said that he'd seen car crash victims with lesser injuries. The local MP explained that he couldn't comment on cases which were sub judice, but that he was convinced that incomprehensibly lenient prison sentences for violent crimes did nothing to deter violent criminals. The Judge was unequivocally harsh in his summing up, and Charlie Grisham was sentenced to a six months jail sentence.

A model prisoner he was released in four, but in reality his sentence was to continue in the open prison which his home became. Charlie had naively assumed the he would return to employment with C.B.F., if at a lower level, but this was not to be. They were still smarting over the negative publicity which the case had brought them, and jokes about the medical insurance that was now included in their furniture warranty and the boxing ring in the customer service department, to mention but a few, were wearing thin.

That was when he discovered that a prison record, compounded by a lack of references, made finding alternative employment virtually impossible. He was becoming a TV couch potato, and he acquired a couch potato girlfriend. Mary Boyle, overweight and poorly educated, had a hobby. She was always on a diet. Charlie saw it as a hobby because she never actually lost any weight, at least not for any length of time. One day as he lay slouched on the settee watching afternoon T.V. he saw an advert for yet another new diet and he suddenly grasped the true beauty of the slimming business. Here was a product whose price bore no relationship to the amount of product supplied, which appeared to be immune from any legal redress when it didn't work, and whose outrageous claims never seemed to be seriously contested. Charlie gave up afternoon TV and worked on his business plan for a diet product to woo the nation and make him rich in the process. Several months later his business plan was ready and the only pounds he planned to remove from his customers would be from their wallets.

The money back guarantee if you didn't reach your target weight in a mere eight week period was the sales closer. The customer purchased dry finger biscuits and vitamin enhanced dips and ate the stipulated number per day for eight weeks, just two months. Provided you stuck to the diet you would either achieve remarkable weight loss or have your money refunded. If you couldn't stick to the diet for eight weeks you weren't taking it seriously. It was marketed as The Skinny Dippers Weight Loss Programme. In some third world countries, people living on similar rations were of serious concern to the International Red Cross. Charlie informed his financial backers that after three weeks the most ardent dieter would be queuing up at MacDonald's for a Big Mac. However teenage girls can be paranoid about their weight with unforeseen consequences. As the National Health Service became involved and anorexia became a household word in Britain, Charlie Grisham became the subject of a vicious hate campaign in the press and social media.

Charlie and his ill-gotten gains, which were considerable, moved to Marbella where he laid low until the furore back in Britain had died down and new scandals had come to the fore. It was two years before he returned quietly to England, the sleepy town of Winkford to be precise, and began to reinvent himself. Charlie Grisham became Sir Charles Grisham. He rewrote his past and confirmed it with the aid of social media, now his ally, while his generosity to local charities cemented his standing in the local community. He invested his remaining funds in property just before property prices soared and his portfolio was now worth millions. He had achieved his ambitions and was reaping the reward.

Now after years of keeping women at length, he had met the woman of his dreams and, although it was complicated, he felt as happy as any sixteen year old with his first crush. Who could have guessed that the death of his mother in a nursing home could put it all at risk?

A phone call to Stanley Bryant revealed that his friendship with his wife Sarah gave him no influence with the Chief Constable whatsoever. His next phone call was to his solicitor and he had just concluded it when the police car arrived and DI Jones informed him that his presence was required at Winkford Police Station for questioning. Charles asked if he might drive there himself as he didn't want anyone to get a false impression. C. S. Donovan was happy to oblige with this request. As he had been drinking, the interview was postponed until the following morning when he duly arrived at the station with his solicitor and was formally read his rights. C.S. Donovan led the interview himself. The case against Grisham was so flimsy it was in danger of falling apart in the interview, never mind in front of a defence barrister. It was an observation made by his solicitor, and one which Donovan found hard to refute. Grisham was not alone in fitting the suspect's description; he was the victim's son, and by all accounts a caring one. He gained nothing from her death, and his method of entering and leaving the building remained a mystery. The only evidence against him was his lack of an alibi. He couldn't even claim to be at home alone because the police had established that he wasn't. Where was he? Grisham refused to say, and knowing that he couldn't be held indefinitely, waited to be released.

John Donovan had one last card up his sleeve. The Winkford constabulary received an assignment that was as urgent as it was unusual. He started the briefing by solemnly asking if everyone was familiar with an old T.V. series 'Dad's Army'. By six o'clock a lineup of ten men had been assembled in Winkford Police Station. Two could reasonably have entered a Captain Mainwaring look-alike competition, one being Charles Grisham who was forth from the left. The other eight could best be described as middle aged, balding, and overweight. James Berkley, who was now being accorded the courtesy afforded to a star witness, surveyed the scene. He walked back to the group of police officers watching him and said emphatically. 'It wasn't one of them.'

The following day Chief Superentendent Donovan received a phone call from Chief Constable Bryant. He was concerned by the lack of progress. He wanted the Pillow Case murderer behind bars before he struck again. He wanted every member of staff and every resident at Morderton Manor interviewed again. That was where both murders had taken place and it was a secure building at night when the crimes had been committed.

C. S. Donovan sat in front of the entire pillow case task force.

'We've been wrong-footed by the sexual activity and the D.N.A,' he began. 'We have to start again. We have a witness and a good description. So where do we start. We've been looking for an assailant who bears a resemblance to the actor Arthur Lowe who may not be familiar to all of you; the late Arthur Lowe who died years ago.' He paused before adding, 'so we've reluctantly removed him from the list of suspects.'

He waited for the laughter to subside before reverting to his serious demeanour again.

'Maybe we should be looking for someone who resembles Charles Grisham. There has to be a motive, a connection between the killer and the victim. Maybe it's a family connection. Find out if he has any brothers, cousins, uncles, who bear a family resemblance and had a motive to want the old dear dead; and check all the friends and family of Sophie Delouche. Did any of them know the Grishams? There has to be a connection. How did the killer get in and out of the building without being spotted? How did he get in and out of the building? It was locked and there's no sign of forced entry? Check the relatives of all the residents. Question any middle aged males who visited the Home on those days.'

However Henry had covered his tracks and the only name in the visitors register was Audrey's. He remained outside the police radar. After answering a few questions from the troops, C.S. Donovan brought the briefing to a close.

'Of course it's just possible that the killings were totally random. If that's the case we're in trouble.'

Henry continued to follow the evolving police investigation through the press coverage of the case. Since the story broke it had filled the columns of the Surrey Echo and the Winkford Chronicle, but with the shock conclusions which were drawn from the second autopsy on the body of Sophie Delouche, several of the nationals were now running the story on a daily basis. He distanced himself from Morderton Manor and kept his head low. His greatest concern was that a member of the staff there might tie him to the crime, particularly the young receptionist, Sylvia, and Mrs Lloyd-King who was apparently leaving when a replacement had been recruited. He wondered how easily they might all be despatched to an early grave, but it was a fleeting thought quickly discarded. Avoiding the retirement home had become imperative. It was reported that all the residents and staff at the retirement and nursing home were to be interviewed again, and the spotlight on Mordington Manor meant that any further fatalities would attract close scrutiny. In any case it appeared that a trip to Canada by the Hollingsworths was unlikely to be repeated in the near future. However, his overriding concern was that James Berkley was once more resident in Morderton Manor and Charles knew that any future contact with him would be disastrous. The game would be up. If Mother did eventually take up residence in Morderton Manor she'd be seeing no more of Henry than Dotty Henderson. Henry settled back into his old routine. A quiet, middle aged accountant, he went to work each day, passing no comment on the biggest news story to hit Winkford since Charles the First spent a night there during the English Civil War. He would calmly wait for the press to lose interest as the supply of new victims dried up, and the police to lose hope as the supply of leads dried up. Mother would be at the top of the vacancy list but there was no time table for the next vacancy. Given the age and health of the present occupants it could be in the not too distant future, but Henry was not confident that Mother wouldn't be wandering around their house in her birthday suit looking for Dotty Henderson for some considerable time to come, pushing Audrey ever closer to some form of breakdown. Furthermore, if press reports were to be believed, Morderton Manor was no longer the retirement home of choice for the Winkford elite. It would be acceptable to find mother an alternative institution in which to spend her twilight years, but enquires had established that they all had much longer waiting lists than Morderton Manor. Against all the odds, it now offered the best chance of getting his life and marriage back to normal. He took some comfort from a report in the Echo that, due to the enduring use of the name Murderton Manor locally, combined with the proposed tawdry film planned by Black Dog Productions; new enquiries by prospective residents had dried up. However, as yet none of the current residents showed any desire to leave by any form of transport other than a hearse. Henry was resigned to an uncertain future

That could have been the final chapter in the pillow case had fate not provided a further twist. Sir Charles Grisham, son of the diseased woman and a dead ringer for Captain Mainwaring, had been summoned to Woking Police Station and was helping the police with their inquiries. If press reports were to be believed, he had a problem with his alibi. As Henry began to recover his optimism Audrey unwittingly showed him the way forward. Over coffee with Beverly Andrews and Heather White the conversation turned to Mother who had entered the kitchen wearing only a hat and scarf and informed them that she was about to go shopping for a matching handbag. After contemplating the future that possibly awaited them all, and wondering if they would all end up with breasts which resembled out of date pita breads, Beverly mentioned that since the death of Linda Grisham, Edward Whitelaw's mother-in-law, Kathleen Frobisher, had taken up residence in Morderton Manor. The family were apparently very happy with her care, regardless of its gruesome recent past. When Audrey recounted this to Henry, the answer to the conundrum of how to expedite the death of a Morderton Manor resident without raising suspicion just came to him, so simple, so subtle, and so satisfying.

If Edward Whitelaw's mother-in-law was now a resident of Morderton Manor, then only a woman called Elizabeth Arnold stood between mother and the next vacancy in the first floor, and she was waiting for the imminent death of a nameless but dying occupant. Henry didn't need to expedite the deaths of any more residents in the home. He just had to expedite the death of Elizabeth Arnold.

Chapter Eight

Henry knew nothing about Elizabeth Arnold other than that she didn't reside in Morderton Manor and her premature death would not be associated with that address. He also knew that speed was of the essence. Elizabeth Arnold had to be eliminated before she became a resident there, and the dying resident she would be replacing was due to meet the grim reaper sooner rather than later. Mother had to take her place. In a worst case scenario the next natural death on the first floor, after the one which was imminent, could be years away. While it was now acceptable to offload Mother into an alternative Nursing Home, the waiting lists were, in Henry's opinion, bordering on criminal. Only Elizabeth Arnold stood between the Hetherington-Busby's increasingly dysfunctional existence and getting their old life back. Henry booked a week's holiday with immediate effect. He felt buoyed up and happy as he looked forward to tracking down his next victim and making a reconnaissance of the next crime scene.

Finding her address was easy. It was in the phone book. Even better, while there were other Arnolds in it, there was only the one E. Arnold. He realised that his task would have been more difficult proportionally to the amount of names he would have had to check, and time was not on his side. Henry's confidence rose. He drove up George Abbot Hill, past the imposing residences which included that of Sir Charles Grisham until he came to the home of Elizabeth Arnold. He drove past it and parked out of sight of the house before walking back down to it. Small by the standards of most of the mansions he had passed; it had however an elegance and refinement that would have made it stand out in any location. Elizabeth Arnold was obviously quite a prosperous woman.

Henry quickly realised that a reconnaissance of the property was going to be much more limited than that of Morderton Manor. For a start, her house on George Abbot Hill didn't border a golf course. It was however surrounded by an eight foot wall with electronic gates. The red metal box situated alongside an upstairs window suggested a sophisticated alarm system. Henry noted the name of the alarm company, Fortress Security. He walked back up the hill and phoned them from his car. He was immediately put through to the sales department who assured him that it would be no problem for a salesman to visit him the following day to discuss a suitable alarm system for his home. Henry then drove down the hill and parked his car within sight of Elizabeth Arnold's house. He waited to see who visited. No one did. Around seven-thirty he headed for home feeling that he had made good progress.

Audrey was rarely surprised by anything that happened in the Hetherington-Busby household anymore, and she didn't even look up from the television when Henry informed her that he was considering updating the burglar alarm. She shrugged and mentally noted that it was probably a blessing that they had been denied the joys of children. The Hetherington-Busby's all appeared to lose touch with reality as they grew older, and it was probably hereditary.

The salesman from Fortress Security found Henry to be a serious and attentive client, looking for a high end system of the type used to protect the homes on George Abbot Hill. Henry discovered that all of their alarms were activated in the same way. They were triggered when beams of light, invisible to the naked eye, were broken, and they protected as many doors and windows in the building as the client wished to pay for. The system was remotely controlled from Fortress Security's head office and only they could deactivate it. It was, as the salesman proudly informed him, tamper proof, and if every door and window was protected, foolproof. But was it? Henry informed him that he wanted to consider the options before making a decision, and the salesman returned to the office with the news that a top of the range sale was in the bag. Henry now knew just how sophisticated the alarm system at number 60 was, but he was sure that he had spotted its Achilles heel. The trick lay not in evading the alarm system, but rather in setting it off in such a way that it would both appear accidental and impossible to reset immediately. He smiled as he considered the ingenious plan which was developing in his fertile imagination. You had to think outside the box.

The following day Henry was parked within view of Elizabeth Arnolds home as he tried to formulate a plan which would make his theoretical plans feasible. He arrived early and had a long but fruitful day. He ascertained that Elizabeth Arnold lived alone with her cat who, like her owner, was in his twilight years and spent a good part of his days watching the world go by from the top of the eight foot high garden wall. The trees on the inside of the wall which allowed her cat to climb on to it would aid an intruder climbing into the garden, and they also cast a shadow where the street lights would have otherwise provided some illumination. Furthermore, while Elizabeth Arnold was a spritely woman who took a constitutional walk every day, she was slightly built and would be easily overpowered. As evening approached he felt that it had been another productive day.

Percy Smart walked up the hill with a golden Labrador and a smartly dressed middle aged woman. On seeing Henry he waved and crossed the road towards him. Henry had been his accountant before he had sold his jewellery business two years earlier and was now accountant to the new owners. He opened the car window, was introduced to Percy's wife Eve, and exchanged a few pleasantries. If Percy had expected Henry to explain why he was parked there, he was to be disappointed because Henry could think of no good explanation. His customary mental agility was to desert him again as approximately an hour later they walked back down the hill and Henry was still there. This time a wave sufficed as Henry cursed his bad luck and lack of foresight. At around seven-thirty when he was preparing to leave, Eve Smart walked up the road towards him again. She gave a puzzled look in his direction and the briefest of acknowledgements as she walked by. He realised that he had unwittingly linked himself to the scene of his next crime and drove off considering the possible implications. The following morning Henry sat in his study all too aware of his tight time schedule, and started to formulate his action plan. As yet he had no idea how he was going to scale the eight foot wall around the garden. He had a rough idea of how he might exit it but bearing in mind his age, shape, and fitness, it was a gamble. He knew a cat resided at the property so presumably there was a cat flap. As the back door was not visible from the road it had to remain a presumption, but it was absolutely critical to his plan. The windows had large panes of glass so accessing the building once the alarm system was out of action should be quite feasible. The woman was slightly built and lived alone so her demise should be easily accomplished. Henry had considered other methods of dispatch which would have cut any links with the pillow case but they made him feel quite squeamish. While other serial killers may have happily stabbed or strangled, Henry found the very thought repugnant. He was, and always would be, a pillow man. Henry sat at his desk and started to put flesh on his skeleton plan. The following day he was up bright and early. He had formulated a plan which, though sketchy in places, was in Henry's view, fit for purpose. He drove to the Wey Retail Park at West Byfleet and just half an hour later he was leaving Pampered Pets with a bird cage and bird seed. He put them into the boot of his car and headed for the High Street and the Arnold Angling Centre, where he purchased a large fishing net and a thermos flask. His next port of call was a large D.I.Y. and home improvement centre in Woking. As he queued at the checkout, he realised that he was failing miserably in his attempt to remain inconspicuous.

'Working tonight are we,' the woman on the cash desk asked him with a wide grin. 'We used to do a nice line in balaclavas, but once the Ripper Gang were kitted out sales dropped off.' Henry just grinned as he paid for the light weight telescopic ladder, the rope, the glass cutters, and two kitchen plungers.

When he returned home Henry considered his position. If he continued on the path he had mapped out it was quite possible that he would find himself linked to the crime. The Smarts could place him at the scene of the crime acting suspiciously, but they were unlikely to relate their tubby, middle aged, ex-accountant, to a complex crime requiring the physical capability of a younger, athletic man. Then there was the woman on the D.I.Y. checkout. Would she connect him to a death on George Abbot Hill if it was found to be suspicious? Again the same logic would apply. He just didn't fit the profile of the person whom the police would be looking for. Lastly there was the motive. Henry's motive was so obscure that it was unlikely to be discovered other than in a psychiatrist's chair, and he had no intention of ever occupying one of those.

The sensible course of action would be to walk away from the plan and its potentially disastrous consequences. He could put Mother on another waiting list and wait for nature and the circle of life to secure her place there in the fullness of time. Henry weighed up the odds and persuaded himself otherwise. For Henry it was no longer about Mother, no longer about an increasingly resentful and unhappy Audrey. Horsey Hetherington was going to claim his birthright. He would be the son of the fictitious father he had created as a child, embellished throughout his life, and now almost believed in. His plan was ingenious and daring, and Henry was going to carry it through.

Chapter Nine

The following morning it rained. Audrey was surprised to see Henry dressed in waterproofs and wellingtons and staring out of the kitchen window. Henry was not a keen gardener and considered mowing the grass on a bright summer's day to be an unwelcome chore.

'Gardening,' she said perplexed.

'No,' replied Henry irritably. 'It's just a little project I'm involved in and I want to keep it to myself for the moment. Not sure how it's going to pan out,' he added by way of explanation.

As Audrey made her way to the kettle she saw a fishing net leaning against the kitchen units and a bird cage and a packet of birdseed on the worktop. She made no comment other than 'would you like a cup of tea?'

Once the shower had passed, Henry put a plateful of birdseed close to the side of the shed and waited to see if the birds that frequented his garden would be enticed by an early lunch. It wasn't long before he got his answer. Two little finches looked around warily, probably on the 'if it's too good to be true' principle, but soon moved to the edge of the plate and tucked in. Henry smiled in satisfaction and moved to phase two.

That afternoon Beverly Andrews from the Women's Institute, one of only a handful of women whom Audrey considered real friends, was popping in for tea. Audrey was a very private person but she was in crisis. She felt tense, heading for an emotional breakdown, and for the first time in her life she felt the need to confide in someone. That someone was going to be Beverly Andrews.

Audrey cast her eyes around the lounge with an increasing sense of despondency. The carpet was blue, the suite was a darker blue, and the curtains contained several shades of blue. The wallpaper was a subtle stripe, a blue stripe. She stared at the picture which held pride of place above the fireplace, a large print of Monet's Water Lilies. It stirred no memory or emotion in her, but it was blue. She had always assumed that this was the stepping stone to a grander home with an impressive postcode. However the future, like the lounge, seemed blue.

But what was really frightening was watching safe, dependable, boring old Henry morphing into what? She couldn't even speculate. It was as though she had been living with Mr Jekyll for years and suddenly Mr Hyde was making an appearance.

Everyone deals with stress differently she thought. She was becoming irritable and moody, but had Mother tipped mild mannered Henry over the edge. It was a shocking thought, but his behaviour was becoming positively abnormal.

Tears rose to her eyes and she struggled to force them back.

Beverly looked positively bewildered.

'It doesn't sound much like Henry.'

There was a long pause.

'Are you sure you're not imagining it,' she said doubtfully. 'Maybe he's having an affair, some sort of midlife crisis. It does happen. You read about it all the time.'

'He's not having an affair,' Audrey said through clenched teeth. 'He's just lost the plot.'

'How can you be so sure?'

A silence followed while a picture of bespectacled Henry, short and rotund with a ruddy complexion and balding hair, came into Audrey's mind.

'Because it takes two to have an affair,' she replied curtly.

'It's often the ones you least expect,' Beverly continued. 'Some women just need company and companionship.'

'If they're that desperate they'll get a dog,' Audrey replied in exasperation.

Henry was soon to realise that there was a pattern developing in the execution of his plans. As with his Morderton Manor exploits, problems became apparent with phase two. When Henry, armed with his fishing net, walked stealthily towards the shed and plate of birdseed, the blackbird that was enjoying its unexpected lunch looked up. If it considered whether this was either a harmless eccentric, or a dangerous predator, it obviously considered the second option a possibility and flew into the trees. Given Henry's recent history this was a reasonably perceptive conclusion. Henry stood to the side of the shed until a solitary blue tit made its way hesitantly towards the birdseed, but it soon became apparent that it was not going to complete the journey while he remained there. He decided to opt for shock tactics and employ the element of surprise. The blue tit proved to be remarkably quick and agile, while Henry was neither.

Audrey looked out of the kitchen window. Her husband was chasing a bird around the garden with a large fishing net. Her mother-in-law was naked in the lounge, looking for a Patsy Cline LP in the general area of the CD player. She made a mental note that if the postman turned up in a onesie, she would drive straight to St. Peters Hospital and book herself into the psychiatric ward. Mother was bad enough, but now Henry appeared to be following her down the road to cuckoo land in the fast lane.

After Henry's bungled kidnap attempt, the queue for lunch from the feathered fraternity dried up. Half an hour later it started to rain again and he returned to the house, deflated, and pondering the fact that he needed a bird to set off the burglar alarm at number 60, George Abbot Hill, but couldn't catch one. He concluded that the obvious answer was to buy one. With bird cage deposited in the back seat he headed once more for the Wey Retail Park and Pets at Home. However, they didn't stock them and could only suggest that he buy one on line. Henry turned to Google and Google did not disappoint. There was a dealer in Camberley, only half an hour away. Henry phoned the dealer and very pleasant woman answered the phone. She assured him that he would find a suitable pet among the fifty plus hand reared birds that they had for sale, all of which came with four weeks free insurance and were treated with mite spray. Henry arranged to visit them the following evening, but as he thought about it, once again the obvious solution didn't stand up to closer scrutiny. The bird's role was to be a simple one; to fly through the cat flap and set of the burglar alarm. This in turn would cause the security company to switch it off once it was established to be a false alarm. A chaffinch flying around the kitchen would probably raise the question, 'how on earth did that get into the house?' The reaction to a budgerigar or a lovebird flying around the kitchen would undoubtedly raise the same question, but with a very different reaction from those charged with maintaining the security of the residence. Henry concluded that the security company was unlikely to accept that a stray parrot in the kitchen was not worthy of further investigation. Furthermore, he realised that, as a very limited number of outlets sold lovebirds, budgies, and small parrots, they would be eminently traceable. Once more it was brought home to Henry that, as with all complex endeavours, the devil was in the detail.

An answer to his conundrum was provided by the most mundane of interventions. Audrey called him on his mobile phone requesting that he bring home a carton of milk. This necessitated a visit to the local corner shop which was not actually on a corner and bore the impressive title of 'The Ed Sanji Emporium' above its door. Ed looked like an Indian, dressed like an East End pimp, and spoke with a broad Yorkshire accent. Everyone knew him, everyone liked him, and he attempted to carry every saleable item that any of his customers could possibly want, in any circumstances, within the confines of his small shop.

The sky was dark and ominous and the light rain was getting heavier as Henry parked his car outside. He went straight to the chilled food area and picked up a carton of semi-skimmed milk. As he turned to walk back to the counter there was a clap of thunder and the sound of heavy rain battering against the roof. He decided to give the rain a chance to abate before braving the elements and returning to his car. Various forms of shelving were compartmentalised into specific product areas, each crammed to capacity with a seemingly random selection of stock, including books, D.I.Y., gardening, and electrical. Even flat pack furniture. As Henry slowly made his way down the aisles he came across a young girl filling up the shelves. A box of plastic footballs on the floor had several shelves containing a selection of cheap toys above it. Above that was a selection of ornaments for a fish tank and on the top shelf there was a selection of picture frames. This was all partially obscured by a revolving stand containing videos. Chardonnay, as her name badge revealed, was filling the gaps in the stand with little if any enthusiasm. Definitely not the sparkling variety thought Henry.

Videos! Did people still buy videos? He glanced at the selection on offer. He heard his sharp intake of breath, felt his heart beat faster. A pair of penetrating blue eyes were staring at him from the superhero on the cover of one of them, his face obscured by a mask. Dressed in a figure hugging black rubber leotard and matching leggings, his arm rested affectionately on the shoulder of a young boy whose leotard and leggings were in vibrant red with a contrasting green cloak.

Henry left the shop positively elated. With a spring in his step he headed for the door, undeterred by the pouring rain outside.

Bats were the answer. Snakes may have left Henry a quivering wreck but bats held no terror for him. Bats hung upside down on the ceiling when they weren't chewing fruit or sucking the blood from some unfortunate dumb animal. Henry wasn't sure which, but it was immaterial. How easy would it be to catch one in a fishing net? Simple; of that Henry felt sure. He not only had a vague memory of thousands of them darting around a cave in an old T.V. documentary, he had personal experience of hundreds of them swarming above his head like a scene from some primeval fantasy. Catching one would be like catching a fish in a shoal of mackerel. The problem would be not netting too many. He only needed one.

If there was one question which every schoolboy in his class at Pinewood School would have been able to answer, it was where do the bats hang out, or literally just hang?

It was Greywell Tunnel on the Basingstoke Canal. A school trip to King Johns Castle at Odium in Hampshire, a forty minute drive by coach, had left an indelible memory with each of the children there, and Henry was one of them. To the twenty-four fifteen year olds the ruins of the small castle had been underwhelming, but a quick visit to the disused tunnel ten minutes further along the canal as dusk was falling had moved every child present. As they approached the tunnel they became as silent as their surroundings. It wasn't just the number of bats entering and leaving the tunnel, it was their speed, sudden changes of direction, and their silence. It was eerie; a scene from some distant, dark, and prehistoric land, far removed from leafy Surrey. Some felt a sense of unease, some a sense of alarm. Some were transported to Transylvania, a few to Gotham City, while the majority just stared in awe. Henry hadn't thought about the tunnel in almost thirty years, but now he was going to pay it a second visit.

As dusk fell Henry drove into the car park of The Mill House. He ordered a pint of Hampshire Rose and waited until he felt that those walking and cycling along the canal footpath would have dwindled to a trickle with the approach of darkness. He drove to the canal, only four minutes away, and parked by the side of the road. There were only three other cars there. Henry collected his bat catching equipment from the boot of his car and headed for Greywell Tunnel. He must have presented a strange sight to the last of the canal-side strollers as he walked along the towpath with a rucksack on his back and carrying a large fishing net and a bird cage.

Darkness fell swiftly. As the light faded and the canal became gloomy, an eerie stillness fell over the landscape with only the gentle flow of the canal breaking the silence.

Between the path and the canal was a bank of green foliage higher than his waist, while on the other side a barbed wire fence and trees created a formidable barrier to the fields beyond, and he began to feel a growing sense of unease as he walked along the path in the gathering gloom. He came to Kings Johns Castle as an almost full moon broke through the blanket of cloud above him. Its stone walls now gleamed in the moonlight and he saw it with fresh and appreciative eyes. He stared at it until the moon once again disappeared and it became a dark and brooding shadow in the darkness before continuing on his way to the tunnel. In the rapidly fading light he saw the bats flying in and out of the man-made cave which they had colonised. Bats held no more terror for Henry than rats or spiders. He retrieved his torch from his pocket and quickly realised that carrying both the birdcage and the fishing net in his other hand was no mean feat. He took one step down from the path towards the tunnel entrance and realised that another step would probably end up with him swimming in the canal. There were no man made steps, only rocks that had been worn by decades of boots clambering on to them. The incline was steep and getting down to the tunnel entrance would have required care if one was carrying nothing at all. He climbed back up again and considered the problem. He made his way down to the tunnel entrance cautiously with the fishing net in one hand and the torch in the other. He would have to transfer his bat to the bird cage on the path. He entered the tunnel. The moon made an opportune appearance again and light reflected off the canal illuminating the entrance. Henry felt a twinge of apprehension.

On the school trip they had remained on the path and for the first time he was seeing the inside of the tunnel. The footpath down the side of the tunnel was very narrow and a few metres in there was a metal grid which prevented further access to the public, while allowing the bats to fly through. The bats were numerous and flew incredibly quickly, changing direction at full speed. Hitchcock's 'The Birds' briefly came to mind. This totally illogical thought was quickly followed by another more pertinent one. Catching a bat would not be easy. As he surveyed the ceiling the moon became obscured by cloud again and he found himself in almost total darkness. He moved back to the entrance of the tunnel and waited for the moon to reappear. After what seemed a considerable period of time it re-emerged from the clouds and the area was bathed in a dim light once more. It was getting colder, he was feeling uneasy, and the number of bats in the tunnel had depleted noticeably. The fishing net proved to be surprisingly unwieldy while the bats proved quick and nimble. After ten minutes he was tired, sweating profusely, and acutely aware that he had almost fallen into the canal. He moved outside the tunnel and climbed up to the path again for a short rest.

It was half an hour later when he returned to the tunnel to find that it was now almost devoid of bats. His initial reaction was to call it a day and come back earlier the following evening. However, he had a deadline to meet and while he didn't know exactly when it was, he knew that the death in Morderton Manor was imminent, and Elizabeth Arnold's demise had to precede it. For all he knew the last rites might be being administered on the first floor at this very moment. Time was of the essence. Henry climbed back up to the path again and opened his flask of soup. It was going to be a long night, but eventually the bats would return and he would catch one.

He was soon to be introduced to the sights and sounds of the night which few see or hear. A hedgehog walked past him purposefully, only stopping for a moment to stare at him before continuing on his way. He could hear an owl hooting somewhere in the distance, but clear in the symphony of sounds which broke the silence of the night. A fox poked its head out of the trees before quickly returning to them again. Henry found himself enjoying his night time vigil. He felt a calmness and contentment that he had not experienced for some considerable time. When he saw the grass to his left move he watched spellbound in anticipation. He was becoming enthralled by the creatures that inhabited the darkness. It moved slowly through the long grass towards him and he threw a piece of bread in front of it more in hope than anticipation. As the slow worm's head emerged from the grass, Henry froze. He knew what it was and he knew that it was harmless, yet he was consumed by a blind panic which was as debilitating as it was irrational. By the time the slow worm had slid back into the long grass again, affording Henry scant attention, he was sweating more profusely than when he had been attempting to catch a bat in the tunnel. He felt shaken, his heart was pounding, and he took some time to regain his composure. He picked up his equipment and headed back to the car. Henry never visited King Johns Castle or Greywell Tunnel again.

By the time he arrived home he was totally exhausted. Audrey and Mother were both in a deep sleep, and Henry was to join them within minutes of getting into bed. He woke around nine o'clock, uncharacteristically late, and didn't get out of bed until ten thirty. He felt deflated, and not a little concerned. He still didn't possess a means of letting off the alarm system 'accidentally', while even more worrying was the fact that Audrey hadn't even mentioned his unusually late night and even more unusually late morning. Henry had many acquaintances but no real friends other than Audrey. She was more than a wife. She was the soul mate he had never expected to meet, his rock in the uncertain life that he had endured before he met her. He would miss his mother when she went to her final resting place, but more out of duty than sentiment. Life without Audrey didn't bear thinking about. With his twilight years fast approaching, at heart he was still the lonely Horsey Hetherington with an imaginary criminal mastermind for a father. Henry resolved to end Audrey's unhappiness immediately if that was humanly possible. That had to be his priority. He would bring the pillow case to a positive conclusion that night, before his life became a car crash.

He looked out of the window. It was a grey day with the probability of rain to follow. Although his confidence was at low ebb, he was determined to at least go through the motions. After a couple of slices of toast he took the birdcage into the garden and placed a bowl of bird seed in it. A simple ball of string would enable him to close the cage door from a distance. He sat on a garden chair outside the kitchen door with little expectation of success. A few minutes later a chirpy little chaffinch perched on the top of the cage and looked in. After a quick check that the coast was clear, it flew to the side of the cage, and then inside. When Henry pulled the string and shut the door it looked up sharply but then returned unperturbed to its meal. Henry had his feathered accomplice. Somehow Henry didn't feel the sense of elation he should have. In fact his mood could better be described as depressed.

Henry wasn't the only person feeling depressed that morning. Chief Constable Stanley Bryant was also facing a marital crisis. While Henry's marriage had been in a steady but slow decline since the arrival of mother, Stanley's had been hit by a meteorite. He was coming to terms with the realisation that his world was collapsing around him and his life was heading in a very different and unwelcome direction. As he considered a lonely lunch in an Indian restaurant or a Chinese takeaway, the full realisation of what this meant was beginning to dawn on him. He couldn't bring himself to even consider such practicalities as food shopping, or the problems posed by dirty laundry. He had been collating information for yet another report and working his way through his diary when he saw the entry,

'Sarah to Caudwell meeting. Staying over.' She had become a trustee of the Cauldwell Hospice although it was sixty miles away in rural Wiltshire, a decision he had never fully understood. Sir Charles Grisham was chairman of this charity among others, but this one was close to his heart as he had been a prime mover in setting it up. Stanley knew that he never missed a meeting and Sarah occasionally travelled with him if it was more convenient. Yet that had been the night of the Sophie Delouche murder. They had stayed in a local hotel. Surely that gave him a cast iron alibi! He suddenly had a gut churning thought. He looked up the date of Linda Grisham's murder and turned to the diary entries for that day. There it was again. 'Sarah at Cauldwell meeting. Will stay over.' The words from DI Jones debriefing by D S Donovan were ringing in his ears.

'He said that if I pursued this line of questioning Chief Constable Bryant would be very upset. He said it wasn't a threat, just a fact. He repeated that my line of enquiry would make the Chief Constable a very unhappy man.'

Stanley now saw those comments in a very different light. He still didn't quite believe what the evidence was telling him, but when he contacted the White Hart he was told that Sir Charles Grisham had booked into the hotel on both nights with his wife. Such an amateurish mistake but he always phoned

Sarah on her mobile. He would have no reason to contact her through the hotel switchboard.

When he confronted his wife that evening her reaction confirmed his worst fears. It wasn't just the shock of her being unfaithful. She'd been unfaithful with a balding, bespectacled, little fat man, who was constantly being described as a dead ringer for Captain Mainwaring. He was appalled. Instead of sympathy he was likely to be the butt of public derision. What would his work colleges make of it? Chief Constables require respect in order to function. Sarah had never considered her relationship with Charles Grisham as anything other than a prerequisite to entry to his social circle, and was in as much shock as he was. After the mother of all domestics Sarah realised that her position in the marital home was now untenable. She packed a case and drove to her mothers.

That afternoon Heather White's coffee morning was proving a spectacular success. Emboldened by her tete-a-tete with Beverley Andrews, Audrey was feeling a weight lifting from her shoulders. She unburdened herself to the assembled ladies who were spellbound by her revelations. She was not an impulsive person and thought through the possible consequence of her actions, but when the floodgates opened there was no stopping her,

'I've felt like just walking out, but where would I go? Life with Henry was never exciting but it was comfortable, I've no doubt he's devoted to me and I was content; occasionally very happy.'

The ladies tutted sympathetically but were careful not to interrupt her revelations. This had all the hallmarks of a memorable afternoon.

'Then that deranged lunatic came to stay with us, wandering through our lives in her birthday suit most of the time, leaving havoc and turmoil in her wake. People joke about their mother-in-law being a monster but she's so awful she's practically a caricature. Henry was duped into bringing her here in order to protect our inheritance and she'd already spent it.'

She could hear the anger in her voice but made no attempt to curb it.

There was more reassuring tutting.

'She always belittled me and now she wanders around my house naked, like some lewd harlot in a low budget movie.'

Audrey's flow stopped as suddenly as it had started. She looked tired and deflated.

'I've been desperate to talk to someone about it.'

'You sound really depressed, 'said Heather .You need to de-stress. Get Henry to take you away for a weekend.'

'We can't get away from her, that's the problem. Not until we can get her into a nursing home. We may get our allotment before we get rid of her, and apparently that's years away,' she said despondently.

'Well that's the best coffee morning I've been to since Harriot Brown's husband ran off with her brother's boyfriend,' ventured Jenny Brady to Heather White once the others had left.

That evening the Hetherington-Busby's were the only topic of conversation among the women of the Winkford W.I.

Henry loaded up his car and went for a late evening walk. He was dressed in a jacket, trousers, and open necked shirt. Henry only possessed one pair of jeans and they had rarely ventured beyond the garden gate. He had several t-shirts but, as with the majority of his clothes, they had been bought by Audrey, and they had been bought when she was shopping on her own. He didn't feel comfortable in them, and even when gardening, he rarely wore them. Henry's idea of dressing down was not wearing a tie and swapping his jacket for an anorak. When he returned Audrey was sleeping soundly. He sat in the chair until one-thirty before getting into his car and heading for George Abbot Hill. He could think of no good reason for being out all night and would settle for 'couldn't sleep'. He was going to bring the pillow case saga to its inevitable conclusion and was optimistically anticipating success. However Henry's plans relied on several assumptions over which he had no control. It assumed that Elizabeth Arnold was home alone, and she wasn't. It assumed that there was a cat flap in the back door, but he didn't actually know if there was. It assumed that all the neighbours would be tucked up in bed, sleeping soundly, and that there were no random problems which just hadn't been foreseen. Henry was to discover that in the real world, criminal actions have none of the certainties of the crime capers in fictional novels.

Chapter Ten

By one-thirty in the morning Henry would, in normal circumstances, be sound asleep. Once again he was surprised by the number of cars on the road at this late hour. Where were those people going? He was given a clue as to where some of them were headed as he drove up George Abbot Hill. Music was blaring from number 53 which was about a hundred yards from number 60, on the opposite side of the road. The parents of Jeremy Ash had picked an unfortunate weekend in which to take a break, and their eighteen year old son had hosted a party which was proving to be more popular than he had intended. While the neighbours were unlikely to be glued to their windows, this was not an area noted for rowdy late night parties and they were unlikely to be asleep. Henry considered the path of prudence, but he was mentally prepared for the night's exploits. He resolved to continue with caution. He made his way down the hill to number 60 with his haversack on his back, the collapsible ladder in one hand, and the caged chaffinch in the other. He was sitting astride the top of the wall with the birdcage securely placed in the branches of an overhanging tree, pulling the ladder up, when he saw the blue flashing light coming up the hill. He put the ladder back down against the wall again and waited for the police car to pass. To his horror it slowed down and parked on the opposite side of the road. Was it all over already? Had he been spotted and reported? He clambered on to an overhanging branch which offered some concealment as the two police officers got out of the car. With his heart thumping he watched them walk down the road towards no 53. As he sat in the tree and tried to regain his composure, a bedroom light in the house opposite was switched on. The flashing police light had done what the party had failed to do. The neighbours were about to look out of the window. Henry was reasonably well concealed as long as he remained still, but the ladder leaning up against the wall was an altogether different proposition. The only way he could conceal it before the curtains opened was to push it over so that it lay on the ground by the side of the wall. He was now trapped within the confines of number 60 until he could improvise some other means of escape. The couple opposite remained at the window for only a few minutes, but left the curtains open. The flashing blue light on the roof of the police car was obviously seen as an indication of interesting developments to follow. Henry retreated a little further into the tree and waited for the police car to leave. It was at this point that the Jack Russell entered the scene. He trotted round the corner and appeared to spot Henry immediately. He ran to the tree, stared at him with tail wagging, and began to bark furiously. Henry's position was precarious. From being trapped in the grounds of the house he now found himself trapped up a tree with two police officers expected back at the scene at any moment. The dog's owner eventually appeared on the scene, an elderly man in tweeds and a flat cap. He stared silently at Henry, in stark contrast to his dog who was hell bent in drowning out the music from number 53. The neighbours opposite were at their window and staring at the man and dog, although unable to see what it was barking at. It was at this point that the music at number 53 was silenced. The return of the police officers was imminent. Henry said the first thing, indeed the only thing, which came to mind.

'Don't tell them where I am. I've got a twenty pound wager riding on this.'

With no idea who 'they' were, the man seemed to find this explanation entirely satisfactory. He smiled, and in a loud whisper said 'good luck,' before putting a lead on the dog and pulling the reluctant terrier away. Without turning round he gave a wave as he disappeared round the corner. A few minutes later the police returned to their car and drove off.

It was fully ten minutes before a shaken Henry climbed down from the tree with the bird cage and headed towards the back of the house. For the first time in what had been an unexpectedly eventful evening the plan was going to plan. At the bottom of the kitchen door there was a large cat flap. Henry knelt down and held it open. He wished the little bird to which he was becoming quite attached a good flight and safe landing before placing the open cage door up against it. However the chaffinch appeared to share his sense of attachment. It seemed to have lost any desire to escape and showed not the slightest inclination to leave the cage. It was as though he knew that the most likely thing to be on the other side of a cat flap was a cat, and no amount of coaxing would shift him. Henry took the cage away from the cat flap and closed its door securely. What was supposed to be an automatic manoeuvre was now going to have to be completed manually. Henry looked at the cage. It was not as simple as it would at first appear. He had to catch the little bird without it escaping, and if it felt threatened its attachment to the cage might evaporate. Henry was acutely aware that he didn't have a spare and that, with hindsight, bringing more than one bird would have been the smart option. He had allowed himself no margin for error. Using the sleeve of his jacket to cover any gaps in the door, Henry reached his hand into the cage. Even in such a confined space the chaffinch was difficult to catch, but eventually he had it in his hand. Not for long. The little bird proved to be a spirited opponent with a vicious peck and Henry had to stifle a scream as he let go. He retrieved a gardening glove from his haversack before making a second attempt. He caught the bird, pulled it out of the cage, and pushed it through the cat flap as quickly as possible. Henry was still nursing his throbbing hand where the bird had drawn blood when the burglar alarm went off. His little feathered accomplice had successfully completed his part of the mission. Henry now hoped he would end up as a supplement to the cat's diet. He ran from the house and stood in the shadow of a large statue of a nude woman on the lawn. The curtains parted in a room upstairs and he saw the old woman look out. Lights went on in another upstairs room. How did she do that? After what seemed an eternity but was actually under ten minutes, other lights went on around the house, both upstairs and down. The old woman was still peering out of the window. Henry realised that, on the assumption that she didn't have a circus trained cat, there was someone else in the house. Surely the chaffinch would be spotted quite quickly and any sense of a threat would be dispelled from the minds of the occupants, whoever they were. Henry's ingenious plan was no longer on track, but a satisfactory outcome was still feasible. Who else was in the house? How many of them were there? What age and sex were they? If it was her older sister he would be able to continue with a bit of improvisation. On the other hand, if it was a couple of rugby playing nephews, he might as well start looking for an escape route from the garden immediately. This was an eventuality he hadn't allowed for. Henry needed some answers if he was to continue. He stood in the shadow of the statue and hoped her guest or guests would reveal themselves.

Sarah's room was at the back of the house where the music was less intrusive and she was asleep when the alarm went off. At first she thought it was a fire alarm and she grabbed her dressing gown and ran to her mother's room. Elizabeth was under no such misconception and was looking out of the window. Sarah joined her for a few minutes, but Henry was standing in the shadow of the statue, and the garden, dimly lit by a starry sky, appeared deserted.

The phone rang and it was Fortress Security. After a quick run through their security checks and ascertaining who was resident in the house, Sarah was advised that they remain together in the bedroom and wait for the police who would be arriving shortly. However the conversation with the operator from Fortress Security was stiffening Sarah's resolve, and while still talking to him in a hushed voice, she tiptoed across the landing and looked downstairs. It was at this point that the luck which had eluded Henry up until now was about to change. The chaffinch had found its way into the hallway and chose this moment to fly up the stairs. With a smile in her voice Sarah explained that the alarm had been set off by a little bird which had somehow found its way into the house. After a short conversation the operator was satisfied and the police response cancelled. It was now that the genius of Henry's plan came into play. The alarm couldn't be reset until the bird was removed from the house, and Sarah made it quite clear that this would not be happening before morning. After giving an assurance that she would contact Fortress Security as soon as the bird had

74

vacated the premises, the telephone conversation came to an end and she went downstairs. Now that she was sure there was no danger, she felt compelled to check the ground floor. It was at this point that she turned on the garden lights. They had been installed by the previous owners, much younger and fans of late night barbecues. When the garden lights came on, they illuminated the lawn as brightly as Wembley Stadium during a Cup Final. This was a security measure of which Henry had no prior warning. He could now see the old woman at the window clearly, and she was staring straight at him. The shadow had evaporated and he scrambled behind the statue. It was probably several years since the lights had been used and Sarah's mood, as well as the garden, was lightened by the fact that they still worked. She opened the kitchen blinds and surveyed the now brilliantly lit up lawn, but could see nothing untoward. However, Henry could see her from behind the statue and he recognised her. She was a trustee for a local cat rescue charity and Henry was their accountant. She had attended the last AGM, as had Henry, and he was sure that if she saw him the recognition would be mutual. Peering through the legs of the statue he saw her move away from the window. With physical confirmation that there were no intruders in the house, she turned off the garden and downstairs lights and went upstairs to break the good news to her mother. Although Henry had no knowledge of the evolving drama in the house, some God of good fortune was now smiling kindly on him. With the garden once again in darkness Henry, ran to the wall and climbed the tree which was providing him with a comforting sense of security and a panoramic view of both the road and the house. The lights were still on, there was another woman in the house, and his hand wouldn't stop throbbing. On the other hand he appeared to have succeeded in getting the alarm switched off and that had been the stroke of genius which made this enterprise uniquely satisfying. Was he going to walk away from it now? Henry decided to stay put for a while. He could consider his options in the light of any further developments.

Sarah climbed the stairs and went back to her mother's room.

'That's enough excitement for one night,' she said 'Crisis over. We'll let our little feathered friend out in the morning.'

Elizabeth remained by the window. 'He's still in the garden.'

'There isn't a he,' replied Sarah. 'It was just a little bird which has somehow got trapped in the house. We'll open the windows in the morning and I'm sure it will take the first opportunity it gets to fly out. The poor little thing was probably scared witless by the burglar alarm.'

'He's still out there,' repeated Elizabeth. 'I saw him quite clearly. What's more I know who he is. He's that man that the police are looking for; the one who looks like Captain Mainwaring.'

Sarah was somewhere between shocked and perplexed. Was this a portent of things to come? She looked out into the dim outline of the garden but could see nothing untoward.

'What makes you think he's the police suspect for the Morderton Manor murders,' she asked.

'I saw him,' Elizabeth replied with some exasperation. 'I saw him as clearly as I am seeing you.' She turned again to the window. 'He's still out there, I know he is.'

Sarah began to have real doubts about the wisdom of her telephone conversation. Her mother's memory could be both sporadic and a bit random, but she seemed to be in possession of all her faculties this evening and very sure of what she had seen. What to do? She was becoming more concerned with every passing moment. The obvious course of action was to dial 999, but she was the wife of Stanley Bryant, Chief Constable. She had every hope of salvaging her marriage from the mess she had created and the last thing she wanted to do was draw attention to her predicament. Calling her husband, her obvious first contact with the police, didn't seem an option. She came to a decision. Charles lived a few minutes down the road. On this occasion he would have to be her knight in shining armour. Any complications could be ironed out later. She didn't have many options. She informed her mother that she would call a friend who lived nearby, stressing that this was only as a precaution, and walked out of the bedroom to call Charles.

Elizabeth was unimpressed by her daughter calling a friend, and in no doubt that they should be contacting the police. As soon as her daughter had left the room she made the decision to phone Stanley. After all, if you couldn't phone your son-in-law when you found yourself in a life threatening predicament, who could you phone, especially if he was the Chief Constable?

This was to be the second of a series of phone calls that night which would dramatically shape the events of the evening. The first was Sarah's call to Charles Grisham. He was asleep when the phone rang and his initial reaction was to tell her to dial 999 and ask for the police. Apart from it being the glaringly obvious course of action to take when being burgled, he had no inclination to take on the Ripper Gang. Sarah assured him that, based on her knowledge of the police investigation, the Ripper Gang were not involved. She could assure him that the culprit was either a figment of her mother's imagination or the Morderton Manor murderer. He got the impression that this baffling piece of information was supposed to allay his fears. If so it was utterly failing in its objective. He again suggested that calling the police seemed to be the appropriate course of action. Why on earth didn't she phone her husband?

Sarah was determined to keep her domestic difficulties under wraps for the moment. In real anger she told him that he was only a few minutes away. The woman he claimed to be passionately in love with was possibly in mortal danger, and he was concerned to resolve the crisis through the correct administrative channels. What kind of a man, if any, was he? A reluctant Charles acknowledged the fact that he was a man. An unfit, overweight, middle aged man, he thought to himself as he got out of bed. He dressed in the nearest clothes to hand which was an old tracksuit for use in the garden, and left the house.

As Sarah spoke to Charles on the landing, Elizabeth left her vigil at the window and picked up her mobile phone from the bedside cabinet. She considered Sarah's decision to call an elderly neighbour rather than the police to be bordering on lunacy. There was no need to dial 999 when your son-in-law was a Chief Constable. She phoned Stanley Bryant. Stanley had obviously been sleeping soundly and appeared somewhat disoriented when he answered the phone. He quickly became alert when he realised who was calling. As she explained her situation the last vestige of tiredness left him. His instructions were concise and compelling. He reiterated the advice of the security company.

'Stay in your room and wait for the police. They will be with you shortly.'

The conversation was brief and he then phoned Winkford Central Police Station. Shortly after his call two police cars were speeding through the night towards George Abbot Hill.

Charles walked briskly up the hill to number 60 with not a little apprehension. What was going to confront him, the Ripper Gang, the Morderton murderer, or nobody? Was it all the product of an old woman's fertile imagination? The situation which confronted him as he arrived at no 60 was one which he would never have considered.

He heard the siren before the flashing blue light sped into view. The police car pulled up beside him and three policemen jumped out in unison. As they surrounded him a second police car came up the hill towards them at speed and pulled in behind the first one. Their demeanour and questioning was aggressive and accusatory. Charles explained who he was and his reason for being there, but it was obvious that his explanation was falling on deaf ears. He had become used to deference and his hackles were rising.

'Do you know who I am? Sir Charles Grisham.' The emphasis was on 'Sir'.

The sergeant looked pointedly at his scruffy tracksuit.

'Pleased to meet you Sir,' he replied in a voice heavy with sarcasm. 'You bear an uncanny resemblance to the description of the suspect we are looking for. He was described as looking uncannily like Captain Mainwaring from Dad's Army. Has anyone ever commented on your likeness to him? I believe he also liked to be called Sir, but then he did have the appropriate uniform.'

He made a point of looking at the scruffy tracksuit again.

'I think it would be best if you accompanied us to the station while we check out your story.' There was a pause before he added 'Sir.'

Charles waited until the sergeant had finished his monologue before vigorously protesting his innocence of any wrong doing, demanding that they speak to the lady of the house, and threatening dire consequences if he was apprehended, but it was all to no avail.

'Our suspect is a dead ringer for Captain Mainwaring,' explained the sergeant, 'and the only difference I can see between you and Captain Mainwaring is that you're the better actor.'

On that note Charles was bundled into the police car and driven away. As they drove back to the station the sergeant made another crucial phone call. He rang the station to report that the intruder had been apprehended, and that he did bear a remarkable likeness to the photo fit of the Morderton Manor Murderer. The news was immediately relayed to Stanley Bryant who in turn phoned his mother-in-law with the news. She could sleep safe and sound in the knowledge that any threat had been averted.

With the news that the intruder was in police custody, Sarah's thoughts turned to Charles Grisham. Where was he? She had rung him on his landline and on his mobile but each had diverted to voicemail. She had put the electric lights on for a second time and walked to the electric gates but there was no sign of him. Surely he couldn't have just ignored her phone call and gone back to sleep; or had he? Sarah realised that it was possible that she didn't really know him very well.

Charles was at this point demanding the right to phone his solicitor, a demand which was duly granted. He had already concluded that a conversation with the police commissioner's wife would lead to a more satisfactory and speedy conclusion than involving his solicitor and he phoned Sarah. Her state of mind was becoming increasingly confrontational as she got his phone call from the police station. As soon as she heard his voice her frustrations surfaced.

'Where the hell are you?' she screamed down the phone. 'Fortunately the police took our predicament more seriously than you did. If our lives were in your hands we'd both be dead by now.' She paused momentarily before another grievance came to mind. 'Why aren't you answering your phone? You always answer your phone, except of course when we have a deranged, psychopathic, serial killer wandering around the garden. The police have driven from Winkford Central, arrested him, and taken him into custody. You live five minutes away. What's taken you so long? Where the hell are you?'

At this point she ran out of steam and Stanley took the opportunity to reply. 'I'm at Winkford Central Police Station.'

'Were you involved in the arrest,' she asked, her voice softening noticeably.

'Well, in a manner of speaking,' he replied. 'I've been arrested and I'm about to be taken down to the cells. It appears that I'm a dead ringer for the Morderton Manor murderer. Now where have I heard that before? I appear doomed to be forever starring in Winkford's Ground Hog Day. It's getting a bit boring to be honest. I'll pass you on to the local constabulary. Would you have a word with them?'

'Talk to them. I'll talk to them, but not down a phone. I want to speak personally to the moron who's instigated your arrest. I want to see him squirm.'

On that note she ended the conversation and slammed down the phone. This was a side of Sarah Bryant which Charles had not seen before, and for the first time his infatuation with the woman was becoming a bit strained.

Sarah had checked the house. She'd checked the grounds. She'd even checked the road outside. There was no sign of the elusive intruder whom she now doubted ever existed. She informed her mother that she had to go to the police station. The detail was best kept under wraps for the moment. She locked the door as she left the house and the gates as she left the garden. She then drove to Winkford Central Police Station.

Henry had watched events unfold from his vantage point on the branch over the garden wall. He watched as the Captain Mainwaring look-alike was arrested. He watched as Sarah Bryant checked the grounds. He saw the lights in the house go out, and then to his amazement, he saw Sarah drive away from the house. His intended victim must be utterly exhausted by now and she was alone in the house. His irrepressible optimism which was never far from the surface, washed over him. As he picked up the rucksack which contained the glass cutters his thoughts turned to the immediate future. With Mother in Morderton Manor, he and Audrey would get their lives back. He'd celebrate by taking her to the new Turkish Restaurant which had just opened to rave reviews. The pain in his hand was almost forgotten and he was practically skipping as he headed for the large dining room window.

Chapter Eleven

Stanley Bryant was not a happy man. He hadn't been happy for some time but it was work related and that he could cope with. This was different. With his marriage collapsing in front of his eyes he was experiencing the onset of depression. It didn't help that he hadn't seen it coming and was totally unprepared. He was suddenly aware of the downside of having no children. The decision may have been intellectually sound and rational when they were younger; enjoying a largely carefree life style interspersed by exotic holidays, but now was payback time. He faced the stark realisation that his only close companion was Sarah, and with her gone, life was going to become very lonely. He was not a drinking man but he had decided to share that evening with a bottle of Jack Daniels. When Elizabeth Arnold rang him in the early hours of the morning he had been sleeping soundly and felt a bit groggy. He initially thought that he had slept in. He quickly revived as he realised who he was talking to. He listened to her account of the evening's events with a deepening sense of trepidation. He had witnessed life-threatening situations throughout his career, but it was very different when the possible victims were those you held most dear. Stanley's reaction to the phone call from Elizabeth was very different from that of Charles to the phone call he'd received from Sarah. However he had to conform to certain standards so he quickly washed his face and shaved before putting on a suit. The phone call informing him that the intruder had been apprehended instantly negated the need for speed and he relaxed, composed himself, and poured himself a coffee. The Jack Daniels he had consumed precluded him from driving and he now asked for the car he had requested to be delayed. He had already decided to conduct the interview himself and he would now prepare for it at his leisure. The suspect could stew in the cells until he arrived. It would give him an insight into his future accommodation. He drank his coffee, and then went upstairs and relaxed in a hot shower. He dressed leisurely, brought a fresh cup of coffee into the lounge, and called the station. He requested that a car be sent to collect him in thirty minutes time. In his experience, the longer the suspect spent alone in a cell, the more productive were the interviews which followed. He was looking forward to this one.

Sergeant Tom Wilson was cursing his luck. Desk duty on a Wednesday night should be a relaxed evening devoid of incidents. The number of police on night duty since the rise of The Ripper Gang had doubled, but most nights, weekends excluded, were incident free. Tonight had been an exception. The capture of the Morderton Manor Murderer had been the most exciting event that the Winkford police had experienced in as long as he could remember. It was just the tonic they needed to counter the constant gnawing at morale by the unbridled success of the Ripper Gang. Night duty was now seen as the shift of choice by many officers as in practice they spent their time playing cards or darts. Now that Winkfords famous killer was safely locked up in the cells, Sergeant Wilson had a night of paperwork ahead of him. He was a painfully slow writer and hated the endless form filling which accompanied every arrest these days. He was engrossed in his paperwork when an attractive and well dressed middle aged woman approached the desk. She was equally well spoken.
'Would I be correct in thinking that you are holding Sir Charles Grisham in your cells?' she enquired.
'We are holding a suspect who claims to answer to that name,' Wilson replied.' Are you his Brief?'
'I am not his Brief.' The woman's voice was suddenly less friendly. 'I am a friend who wants him released immediately. This is not the first time he has been dragged down to the police station merely because he bears a likeness to a man you wish to question. I can assure you that it's a mistake which won't be repeated.'
'It has long been police policy not to release murder suspects because their friends pop in and ask us to,' he answered dryly. 'If it proves to be a case of mistaken identity

he'll be released in due course. With a full apology,' he added with a broad grin.

'He'll be released immediately.' Her voice was rising. 'I want to speak to the officer in charge. You can tell him that the Chief Constable's wife is at the desk and would like to speak to him.' Wilson was about to look around the room and ask where she was but he thought better of it. She was at best delusional but you could never be sure, and she was very different from the riff- raff that he was used to dealing with. He decided to err on the side of caution and keep the conversation polite. He now just wanted to get back to his report. Unlike this woman he couldn't make it go away so he determined to get rid of her as soon as possible. He informed her that she was talking to the officer in charge.

'I'm surprised you've come to the station. The Chief Constable usually phones. As a matter of a fact he rang earlier. That's when he instructed us to arrest your friend. I'm surprised you didn't know. We find his communication skills to be one of his strong points. It's good to talk,' he added. 'He'll be here shortly. He's going to conduct the interview himself. I've no doubt that when he realises that Mr Grisham is actually a close family friend he'll have him released immediately.'

He suggested that she remain in the seating area until he arrived and he would have a cup of tea brought to her. He was interested to hear what her reason for leaving would be. He had had a feeling it was going to be good. She was indisputable proof that a person could be one sandwich short of a picnic while also as sharp as a knife.

She just stared at him. Could Stanley have done this out of spite? Surely not, but what possible reason could he have for locking Charles up for a night? Was he planning to discuss their affair in a police interview room? Charles would be in a position to ruin him. Was he having some sort of breakdown? When she'd embarked on the occasional fling with Charles Grisham it had been intended as an elevator ride to Winkfords social heights at a time when the staircase was proving infinitely long. Without the interference of a homicidal maniac in their lives it would have remained a secret and no one would have got hurt. What were the chances that some bloodthirsty killer would randomly murder the mother of the man you were having an affair with on one of the very few nights you slept with him, and in doing so deprive him of an alibi? You couldn't make it up. She had never intended to put her marriage at risk and the events which had conspired against her had been impossible to foresee.

Sarah determined to take Sergeant Wilson up on his offer. She would confront Stanley over the arrest of Charles and try to bring him back from the brink before he put his career in real jeopardy.

The wait was longer than she anticipated. Stanley was in no hurry.

Henry looked at the large dining room window and took the glass cutter from his haversack. He started by attaching two kitchen plungers to the glass. He had intended to cut a hole in the window large enough to climb through but the glass cutter he had purchased now seemed a very small and insubstantial tool. He held the blade against the glass and started to cut a large oval section around the kitchen plungers. It took much longer than he had envisaged and he was exhausted by the time he had finished. He paused to recover his breath and surveyed his work. The window had the appearance of having been scratched, but not that badly. He pulled the plungers out towards him, gently at first. Nothing happened. He pushed them away from himself with the same outcome. He slowly increased the force used but to no avail. He gradually increased the pressure until he was pushing and pulling on the plungers with all his strength, but the glass remained steadfastly in place. He was seriously considering looking for a brick or an equivalent when he saw the catch on the side of the window frame. This offered the possibility of opening the window with only a very small piece being cut from the glass. He picked up the glass cutters once more and scored the glass as deeply as possible in a small circle to the side of the catch. Once again the glass stubbornly refused to budge. Henry was running out of options. He looked around for an aid with which to remove the small circle of glass from the window. He walked to the shed but it was locked. He returned to the dining room window and hit the centre of the glass circle with the handle of his torch. He hit it a bit harder. Finally he threw caution to the wind and hit it as hard as he could. The glass shattered, but within the circle. However the glass was not the only thing to break. The light from his torch went out and could not be coaxed back on again. From now on Henry would not just be working in the dark metaphorically. He looked around anxiously. He was sure the noise could have woken the dead, but there was no sign of life from either the house or its neighbours. Henry now had to work in the dim light emanating from the grey sky above. He put his hand through the hole in the glass and towards the window catch. That's when the principles of double glazing were brought home to him. He'd always known how it worked, but he'd never really thought about it. He thought about it now. There was another pane of glass between him and the window catch. Cutting the second piece of glass was to prove much more testing than the first. He was wearing gardening gloves but the area in which he now had to work was very constricting. As he made another circle in the interior pane of glass the edge of the outer pane cut through his glove and sliced the side of his hand. The cut wasn't deep but Henry watched in horror as the splashes of red DNA dropped down the inside of the glass and on to the bottom of the window frame. The significance was not lost on him. There were already two witnesses who had seen him clearly and could identify him. Now he was leaving his DNA all over the crime scene.

'You get less evidence in a game of Cluedo,' he muttered under his breath.

As he broke the second pane of glass with the torch and opened the window he knew he had a momentous decision to make. He could walk away from a failed burglary which would probably be attributed to the Ripper Gang, or he could finish what he'd started; but the evidence against him was undeniable should he become linked to the crime. He climbed through the window and walked across the lounge and into the hallway. He went into the kitchen, put the light on, and wrapped a dishcloth around his bleeding hand while he considered his options.

When the police car chauffeuring Stanley Bryant finally arrived, Sergeant Wilson was waiting in anticipation to see what his reaction would be to the woman waiting in reception. He appeared to know her and be far from happy to see her. In hushed tones a heated argument developed between them. He approached Wilson and enquired whether it was true that the suspect being held in the cells was indeed Sir Charles Grisham. He groaned audibly when Wilson confirmed that this was the name he had given. He asked for an interview room to be made available, but instead of bringing Charles Grisham up from the cells to be interviewed, he went into it with the woman whom, it transpired, was indeed his wife. When they emerged twenty minutes later they both appeared to be in a much improved state of mind.

It hadn't taken long to establish that a comedy of errors had led to the arrest of Charles Grisham. It had taken a little longer to establish that Sarah Bryant was as deeply upset by the outcome of her affair as her husband was upset that the affair had taken place. It took a little longer to establish that neither wanted a divorce and they left the room with the outcome Marriage Guidance Counsellors dream of but rarely achieve.

Sergeant Wilson was then asked to bring Charles Grisham to the interview room where the Chief Constable interviewed him in the presence of his wife, and only his wife. In an era of rules and regulations the whole procedure was proving highly irregular. When the three of them emerged from the interview room, Wilson was instructed to discharge the prisoner. It had been a case of mistaken identity. Sir Charles Grisham decided that he would rather not be taken home in a police car and phoned for a taxi. He looked towards Sarah Bryant as he left but there was no warmth in her expression and no words were spoken.

Sergeant Wilson felt sure that something wasn't right. He wasn't sure what it was, but the nights events were becoming surreal. Were they really going to let a murder suspect walk free because the Chief Constable's wife vouched for him?

'What exactly was he doing in an old ladies garden in the middle of the night?' he asked the Chief Constable.

'He wasn't in the garden. He was apprehended before he got to it. He was going to the house because he was a friend who was coming to her aid. In truth, he would not have been able to get into the house until the electric gates were opened for him. There was no intruder. The occupant is an elderly woman who worries about the Morderton Manor murderer because she is about to move into that establishment. The intruder was the figment of a tired old women's imagination. There was no one in the garden.'

'Oh yes there was.' Wilson's voice lacked any doubt. 'He used a ladder.'

'A ladder?'

'Well someone used a ladder. It's in the report. It's lying against the wall until it gets picked up as evidence.'

The implication of Wilson's words was apparent to them all. They hadn't just arrested an innocent man; they had arrested the wrong man.

'Good God,' Stanley whispered. 'We may be too late.'

Minutes later a police car with Stanley Bryant and three police constables was speeding towards George Abbot Hill with Sarah Bryant in close pursuit, and Sergeant Wilson was phoning Elizabeth Arnold in the hope of finding her alive and advising her to hide until the police car arrived.

Chapter Twelve

Henry's decision was inevitable. He was on a roller coaster with which he had formed such an emotional attachment that he felt compelled to complete the journey, even when common sense dictated that he should get off immediately. He left the kitchen with the dishcloth still wrapped tightly around his hand and climbed the stairs. Once on the landing he stopped for a few minutes while his eyes adjusted to the darkness. It was penetrated just enough by the light emanating from the kitchen for Henry to make out several doors. Only one was slightly ajar and he could hear the sound of heavy breathing coming from the room. Amore perceptive man may have wondered why the door had not been shut but Henry only saw it as a stroke of luck, long overdue. The woman was obviously in a deep sleep and Henry opened the door wider and stared into the darkness. The blackout curtains were highly effective and he couldn't see anything, but he could hear her heavy breathing. Even in the darkness Henry was sure that the task ahead would pose no problems. He moved slowly forward until he felt the foot of the bed. He moved to its edge and took a step towards the sound of steady breathing. In the darkness he heard the hiss. It was a vicious hiss. In his mind's eye he saw the cobra of his nightmares. He saw its venomous fangs strike towards him just as Pasha, Elizabeth's cat, scratched him viciously. He jumped back in terror. He could feel the blood on his cheek. He froze. He couldn't move forward but neither could he move back. He stood rooted to the spot and began to shake uncontrollably. The phone on the bedside table rang. Sergeant Wilson's phone call was to be the last significant phone call of the evening. When the phone rang the woman stirred and Henry came out of his trance. With no attempt at stealth he ran from the room. He ran downstairs, jumped out of the window and ran across the garden. He slowly climbed the tree. He didn't stop for breath until he was sitting on top of the wall utterly exhausted. Only then did he realise that he had left his haversack with his glasscutters, broken torch, and an almost empty flask of coffee, under the dining room window. He couldn't go back for them. He just wanted to get away from the house as quickly as possible. A pair of eyes watched him from the landing window and followed his progress in the darkness as he crossed the garden to the perimeter wall. Pasha had left the bedroom through the partially open door as he did most nights. He appeared to be smiling but that may have been a trick of the light from the kitchen.

Henry was out of condition and utterly exhausted. A lifetime in accountancy hadn't prepared him for this. His clothes were saturated with sweat, his legs felt like rubber, and he was gasping for breath. He jumped from the wall and landed on the ladder below. At first he thought he had broken his ankle but it was just badly bruised. With a sharp pain shooting up his leg every time he put any weight on it, he limped up the hill towards his car. As he slowly made his way round the corner in the road an elderly couple dressed from head to toe in fluorescent green Lycra cycled towards him. He must have appeared a pitiful sight. There was blood on his face, he had two injured hands, and his leg was obviously badly hurt. They both dismounted and asked him if he was ok. He definitely wasn't ok and was even less ok now that they had joined the increasing list of witnesses who could identify him. Who were these people? Why were they out cycling in the middle of the night dressed like giant radioactive grasshoppers? He politely but firmly informed them that he was ok and limped on past them.

It was at this time that the police car from Winkford Central closely followed by Sarah Bryant arrived at number sixty. Sarah opened the electric gates and both cars drove in. As the house was searched and Elizabeth Arnold was being both comforted and debriefed, Henry drove past them down George Abbot Hill, and made his way home.

Audrey had been asleep when Henry arrived home and when she woke up he was asleep which was highly unusual. He had three parallel scratches on his cheek. When he woke up two hours later she discovered that he also had two injured hands which needed bandaging and a badly bruised and swollen ankle. Henry had apparently been attacked by a dog; a Rottweiler to be precise. It was just wandering down the road with no owner in sight, looking for a fight. Henry didn't want to talk about it so she cleaned and dressed his wounds and brought him some tea and toast. It was obvious that he was distracted and his thoughts were elsewhere.

They were. Henry had a problem and it was a big problem. He knew that if he ever became a suspect the game was up. His security from arrest relied on the lack of any link between himself and any of his victims. He did bear a likeness to Arthur Lowe and the police did appear to have tunnel vision with regard to their profile of the Morderton Manor murderer, but he was confident that they were not looking for an unassuming, overweight accountant with no connection to the victims.

Although Henry had been seen by James Berkley, it had been in a dimly lit bedroom, and while the photo fit from his description had borne a likeness to him, the same could be said of numerous other men of a similar age. James Berkley was now residing in Morderton Manor again and Henry had felt that, provided he kept away from there, the threat of his being linked to the murders was an increasingly diminishing one.

Sixty, St. Georges Hill, presented a very different scenario. He had been seen by several witnesses. The man with the dog had been only a few feet away from him and Elizabeth Arnold had seen him in the full glare of the floodlit garden. The couple of rather weird cyclists had engaged in a very brief conversation with him. It was inevitable that one of the witnesses to his being there would cross his path at some point in the future. Winkford was a small town. They would recognise him immediately. It could take months but it could take weeks, even days, and then the game would be up. He had left his D.N.A. all over the crime scene. Then there was the haversack, the glass cutters, and the broken torch. They would have his fingerprints all over them. The inevitable consequence could only be that he would be spending a considerable length of time in jail. Furthermore, he had injured hands, one of which would have benefited from a visit to the surgery, large scratches across his cheek, and he was walking with a pronounced limp.

Henry knew that he now had to leave Winkford and leave quickly; but where could he go? To be totally safe he would have to leave the country. Spain. That's where the criminal classes retired to. Sun and sand; he'd forsake the sex and take Audrey with him. He'd settle for sangria. How to leave for Spain suddenly without it appearing suspicious? That was the question he had to answer and he didn't have much time. Even more important was the problem of Audrey. She was totally unaware of his exploits and he now had to explain his actions and bring her on board as his willing accomplice. Henry recognised a challenge when he saw one, and this was a challenge.

He sat Audrey down. 'I've something important to tell you he said.'

Audrey sensed that his mood was serious and turned off the television. She could learn how to cook Mangalorean Prawn Curry another day. She listened attentively, showing little sign of emotion, as Henry explained how he had attempted to shortcut Mothers entry into Morderton Manor. When he had finished she looked at him with an expression of sympathetic concern.

'So you're the Morderton Murderer.'

She used the calming tone she normally reserved for Mother when she was rambling on about coffee mornings with friends, long departed. She was following the social worker's advice to just agree with everything said. She didn't expect Henry to have forgotten the entire conversation by the time she had made a cup of tea, but she was sure the principle was the same. Henry had been preparing mentally for anything between a verbal onslaught and a mental breakdown, but the idea that he would be confronted by disbelief and concern for his mental wellbeing was a scenario which he hadn't even considered.

'I'm not making it up you stupid woman,' he shouted at her in frustration. 'I need your help to extradite myself from a difficult situation. This isn't one of mother's fantasies. Pull yourself together because this is serious and unlike your Mills and Boon stories it isn't guaranteed a happy ending. You don't appear to appreciate the gravity of the situation we find ourselves in.' He emphasised the 'we'. 'You need to realise that we are facing a very real problem and we need to work together and quickly if we're to evade the possible consequences.'

'Which could be appalling,' he added as he stormed out of the room.

Henry decided that with time at a premium it would be best to let Audrey consider his disclosures at her leisure, while he concentrated on the numerous other tasks at hand. He considered his plan of action. Come up with a reason for leaving the country at very short notice without arousing suspicion, and sort out a Spanish bank account. Resign from Clifton Harrison and sons and tie up any work related loose ends. Put the house on the market and sort out some alternative solution to mother's accommodation requirements. He was acutely aware that selling the benefits of a life in the sun to Audrey was as crucial as it was going to be difficult to achieve. However, it was vital if they were to fly away to safety, and the sooner he was in sunny Spain, the better.

When Henry left, Audrey considered his latest eccentricity. The Morderton Murderer; it had to be the manifestation of some form of mental breakdown, and people didn't get attacked in Winkford, it wasn't that kind of place. Being attacked by a Rottweiler was a first for this sleepy little town. Where had it happened? Henry had been very short on detail and the breed of dog kept as a pet in Winkford ranged from Poodles to Labradors. A Rottweiler was a guard dog. What had it been guarding so successfully from Henry? It all seemed highly improbable.

She felt herself drowning in the cloud of anxiety which was engulfing her, and a troubled frown replaced the look of stoic resignation which had preceded it. Henry's story about being attacked by a Rottweiler in Winkford was preposterous; quite ridiculous. She had always lived in Winkford and she'd never seen a Rottweiler. So who had attacked Henry, and where, and why?

She was viewing his increasingly peculiar behaviour with mounting concern. She had always acknowledged that his fictional father was probably a mental health issue, but it had appeared harmless, although it sometimes manifested itself in unpredictable ways. He had attended the Mayor's Charity Ball, a fancy dress affair where the theme was great men of the twentieth century, as Al Capone. Most of those present had assumed he was a badly dressed Winston Churchill of which there were several in the room, and several of the other offerings were frankly appalling. Two of the Churchills, who inexplicably wore dark glasses, were assumed to be the Blues Brothers, and they hadn't even arrived together. However, he now appeared to have developed a fascination for the small birds in the garden. She had watched with some unease as he had chased them around the garden with a fishing net, but it was a giant leap from developing a fascination for small birds to claiming to be the serial killer at the top of the police most wanted list. At what point did the delusions of a troubled mind become too serious to keep hidden? Was this the point at which his need for help outweighed the dire social consequences which would inevitably follow? She dwelt on the problem throughout the afternoon and a terrible thought entered her mind and started to take hold.

What if it was true?

The more she thought about it the more credible the previously implausible scenario of Henry as a serial killer became. He had been in Morderton Manor on the nights of the murders. His reasons for being there had appeared odd at the time but not as odd as his behaviour when they had got there. He hadn't returned until the following morning on the night of Linda Gresham's murder. Audrey shuddered as the realisation of Henry's iniquity dawned on her. Could he really have murdered two defenceless old women? She felt numb as she considered the probable consequences.

What would the bridge club think? They would undoubtedly become personae non gratae in the Thornton's social set. She

94

would become a pariah at the Women's Institute. The implications of Henry's disclosures were dreadful, too awful to contemplate. Mother's permanent state of naturism and constant verbal drivel, once the bane of her life, paled into insignificance.

Chief Constable Stanley Bryant was discussing the Elizabeth Arnold case with Chief Superintendent John Donovan and he was uncomfortable with the direction in which it was going. As they faced each other across the desk John Donovan was unimpressed by the conclusions reached by his boss and was making his feelings clear. The evidence did not point to a hardened killer intent on murder. The supposed victim was an elderly and physically small woman in her bed. When she was woken by the phone ringing, the supposed assailant had been in her bedroom. He had run from the house as fast as his legs could carry him. In his eagerness to get away he had dropped a tea towel covered with his blood, and had left behind his haversack and its contents. The method of entry and the fact that he'd cut himself in the process didn't point to an experienced criminal.

'His profile is proving markedly different from that of the Ripper Gang,' he remarked dryly

Stanley Bryant remained uneasy with this presumption that the crime was merely an amateur attempt at burglary which had failed, but he had to admit that it did fit the facts. The DNA found at the scene would be put on the police data base until the thief inevitably got caught committing some future crime, but other than that they were too busy trying to catch real burglars to devote much of their already stretched resources to pursuing this one.

Henry limped purposefully into the Winkford Branch of the Santander Bank. It was devoid of customers and he approached the young woman at the counter. He explained that he would shortly be moving to Spain and he wished to open an account with a view to transferring money there. She made no mention of his multiple injuries as she consulted her computer and informed him that she could arrange an appointment for the following Wednesday afternoon. Henry explained that he had hoped to complete the paperwork that day as he was leaving for Spain the following evening. The girl again looked at her computer screen but it remained unmoved by Henry's predicament. When Henry got up to leave she left her desk to seek help and returned shortly to tell him that an appointment could be arranged for four-thirty the following afternoon. This was not what Henry wanted to hear but he concluded that it was the best he could hope for. He had hoped to be flying out the following day but it would be unwise to book a flight before he was certain that his funds had been transferred. It appeared that his departure would now have to be postponed for twenty-four hours. Given the amount of loose ends that had to be tied up, he concluded that the short delay might prove a blessing in disguise.

When he returned home Henry spoke again to Audrey. He realised that bringing her on board was crucial to his bringing his endeavours to a satisfactory conclusion. He justified his homicidal undertakings among the elderly residents of Morderton Manor as being the actions of a caring son and husband. Audrey was appalled to discover that two charming old ladies had died in order to relieve her burden of caring. Henry acknowledged that his motive could be portrayed as selfish. Well, if trying to get the best possible care for your mother was selfish, he would admit to being selfish. It wasn't as though he had killed anyone in the prime of their life; quite the contrary. The Grim Reaper had been on his way. He had merely brought forward the appointment. Audrey had to see it from his perspective.

Audrey had remained silent throughout but appeared more sympathetic than shocked. Henry was delighted. He'd always known she was a good egg; his rock in a crisis. He quickly succumbed to his over-optimism and assumed that Audrey was on board. Audrey may well have been listening in rapt attention to Henry's brief summary of his exploits to date, but she was definitely not on board. She was already facing the realisation that he would undoubtedly be locked up for a very long time. When he left prison he would probably be moved straight into a retirement home himself. He wouldn't be on a waiting list. He was completely mad. He might well be sectioned. If that happened he could end up in a nursing home before his mother. How ironic was that. She would endeavour to get Mother into a Home before him, not that she needed an incentive to get rid of the old bat. They were both barking.

Unaware of her opinion, Henry made his plans with Audrey in a pivotal role. Her part would be crucial in their sudden relocation to Spain without causing undue or vexatious comment. It was sensible for him to leave Winkford at the earliest possible opportunity. Audrey would have to stay behind to organise Mother's retirement home and the sale of the house before joining him. He would be able to guide her but it would be from a distance. His immediate problem was finding an acceptable reason for their sudden departure which would satisfy friends and colleagues. He racked his brains for a reason to relocate, aware that any suggestion of criminality, however tenuous, had to be avoided at all costs; but to no avail.

He turned to Google for help. The move could be explained by some massive lifestyle adjustment involving a change of job. Unlike most criminals on the Costa del Crime, his criminal career had not been financially lucrative. His capital consisted of some modest investments, the unexpectedly depleted proceeds of his mother's house sale, and the impending sale of their own house. While far from destitute he was going to need some other form of income in the future anyway. He scoured the internet with growing despondency. All the jobs available to English speaking employees seemed utterly unsuitable. A deep desire to serve paella or pour pints to the embarrassingly indulgent Brits abroad was hardly going to stand up as the lifelong dream of a middle aged accountant. Organising volleyball competitions or discos on the beach as a holiday rep seemed no more plausible. In desperation he toyed with the idea of always having wanted to sell time shares. But why would you?

He turned to Commercial Properties for sale. Even if he didn't buy one it would give him a valid reason for leaving Winkford to follow a fantasy dream. There was a seemingly endless list of failed businesses for sale, mainly in the retail sector, mundane and uninspiring. He flicked through them dejectedly and there it was. He felt his heartbeat quicken. It was the answer to his prayers. If you're going to tell a lie, tell a big one, and they didn't come much bigger than this. If following a dream was going to be his reason for leaving, then this would be an acceptable, if somewhat eccentric, dream. If it was so crazy, as to be completely implausible, people would believe it. Henry gave a satisfied smile. He needed to get some background. He turned again to Google.

Henry had a busy day ahead and he rose early. He explained to a compliant Audrey that she would have to get Mother into a Home, any Home. The need to impress anyone had long passed. She would also need to sell the house before joining him in Marbella. Audrey dutifully nodded. Her dream destination was Devon, but she shared Henry's overriding concern to keep his homicidal past under wraps. She would concentrate on easing his relocation to the Iberian Peninsula for now. Henry turned to writing to those who needed to know that he was leaving. He started with the firm of Clifton Harrison and sons, accountants. He laughed out loud as he read again his reason for leaving and admired his own brilliance. Once again he wished he could share it with someone. Was his father looking down on him proudly? If only. Even Henry's imagination would only stretch so far. Letters written, he headed for the Post Office. He purchased two books of first class stamps and faced the point of no return. As he posted the letters he knew he was making a momentous decision and now there was no going back.

That afternoon Henry once again limped into the Winkford branch of Santander. After a few moments he was introduced to a friendly young man named Simon who appeared both competent and confident. As with the young lady the day before he didn't appear to notice his scratches, limp, or bandaged hands. Henry began to feel relaxed. He explained that he was moving to Spain immediately and wished to open an account from which he could easily transfer funds to his new location.   Suspicion immediately registered on the young bankers face.

'When are you relocating?' He asked.

'Tomorrow,' replied Henry.

It was obvious that this reply did nothing to allay his suspicions.

'I want to buy a business which has come up for sale,' Henry explained. 'It's been my dream for more years than I care to remember. If I don't get this one I'm unlikely to get the opportunity again.'

'What business is this?' Simon was obviously intrigued.

'A bullring,' replied Henry.

'A bullring,' the young man repeated slowly. He looked around the room. It had suddenly occurred to him that he might be the victim of a reality TV programme. He could see nothing which might conceal a hidden camera.

'You want to buy a bullring?' he asked. He felt that he needed confirmation.

'That's correct,' Henry replied. 'I always wanted to be a matador but I didn't have the height.' He was warming to his theme. 'The bulls aren't bothered but the spectators like their matadors to have a certain stature. However, with a lifetime's experience in accountancy I feel well qualified to open it for business again and make a success of it.'

Simon's eyes started to wander around the room again. 'Will you be looking for finance for this project?' His tone suggested that the business plan would have to be compelling.

'No I won't be needing finance,' Henry assured him, 'just a simple method of transferring funds across.'   Simon now concluded that he was dealing with one of those unique eccentrics which had been a British export since the reign of Queen Victoria.

'Do you know much about bullfighting?' he enquired.

'I certainly do,' replied a beaming Henry. This was the first part, indeed the only part, of his story which was actually true. He felt that, with the help of the knowledgeable Google, he had become something of an expert. He had come equipped with all the necessary documentation and the paperwork which followed was surprisingly quick and easy. He left with not only a bank account in the Winkford branch, but also one in a branch in Marbella into which he had transferred the bulk of his funds. His thanks to Simon were profuse and genuine. At last lady luck was looking kindly on him.

The following morning Henry visited a local travel agent. He booked a single ticket to Marbella and paid the excess for three suitcases. He didn't envisage coming back. When he got home he went through the procedures involved in selling the house with Audrey in some detail, and he then put Mother on the waiting list of every nursing home in a fifty mile radius of Winkford. As they would be in Spain her location no longer seemed important. Once they were settled he would cancel the payments to the home and let them sort out her future accommodation. After all that was their area of expertise. As Henry packed his three suitcases he realised the enormity of what he was doing. He said his farewells to Audrey, happy in the knowledge that their separation would be a temporary one. He assured her that he would only be a phone call away with help and advice as she tied up the loose ends in England. He said good bye to Mother, but she seemed oblivious to what was happening. It had all happened so quickly. It seemed only yesterday that he had been smothering the life out of Sophie Delouche, and so much had happened since then. He stared out of the taxi's rear window. As he watched the lights of Winkford disappear he felt a tinge of sadness. He sped towards Heathrow Airport and an uncertain future.

Chapter Thirteen

Henry relaxed in his chair. It was his birthday and he was alone at his table outside the Honolulu Bar, but that wouldn't be for long. This was the bar of choice for the flotsam that washed up in Marbella from the UK and Europe. They came in varying degrees of shady, but shady they all were, with a tale to tell; a sanitised version of a murky past. Henry's story was up there with the best of them but as yet he'd kept it to himself. The Brits were regulars at the bar and even had their own table. There was an unspoken agreement among the regulars to reserve it for them, and it was only broken by the occasional tourists who wandered in, unaware of this protocol. There were about a dozen customers in the bar which was understated but smart. They were a mixed bunch; everything from a Russian blonde who called everyone darling, to an overweight black man with an accent from Africa and sunglasses that came from Paris or Milan. Diamonds caught the light and sparkled as only the real ones can and several men wore a Rolex like a badge of eligibility.

Around seven a boisterous pack of tourists spilled into the bar bringing discord to its sleepy ambience. However after one drink they moved on, looking for a more exciting destination. The air was warm and the sky was blue. It was only five weeks since he had left Winkford, but England seemed a million miles away. He took another sip of his cold beer. He was settling contentedly into the expat lifestyle.

Audrey seemed reluctant to talk about any reports in the local press regarding the ongoing police enquiries into the Morderton Manor murders or the break-in on George Abbot Hill. It was almost as though she felt that discussing it made her an accomplice. However, he had discovered that the Winkford Chronicle published a weekly summary of local news on their website. He had scarcely looked at the paper in all the years that he had lived there, but he now browsed their website avidly and eagerly awaited their updates. What was being described as a botched attempt at burglary on George Abbot Hill was the Winkford Chronicle's headline news the following week, although it was being stressed that it was in no way associated with the Ripper Gang. A photo fit of the suspect that the police would like to interview was remarkably inaccurate. He was assumed to be a much younger man and, due to his wearing a woollen hat, to have a full head of hair.

For some inexplicable reason the man with the dog thought he was three or four inches taller than he actually was. Elizabeth Arnold's assertion that he looked like Captain Mainwaring was attributed to the widely reported crimes in Morderton Manor. When the cyclists eventually contacted the police two weeks later they only had the haziest of recollections of Henry's appearance other than that he was walking with a limp.

It was a spectacular robbery by the Ripper Gang a few weeks later which effectively closed down the Pillow Case enquiries. The home of the Police Commissioner was burgled while she was at a top secret conference on zero tolerance policing. Amanda Quinn was the darling of the Right in both politics and the press, a rising star with the promise of a remarkable future. She had been known as Mani Quinn since her earliest school days and she had heard every mannequin joke a hundred times. By the time she reached her teens even her school friends were of the opinion that the joke had been flogged to death. They didn't re-emerge until she entered local politics. An attractive woman, her picture often appeared in the press with captions such as 'Dressed to thrill'. Her entry into the hanging debate was an open invitation to change it to 'Dressed to kill'. It continued to be an asset to the spin doctors when she ran for the position of Police Commissioner. With press headlines such as 'Man enough for the job' and 'Best suited candidate for the position', she romped home to become the first female to hold this office. However the exploits of the Ripper Gang on her own turf were beginning to put the love affair under strain. When she herself was burgled the fallout was disastrous. The headlines continued the same theme but with a very different message. 'Mani Quinn caught with her pants down' was a much quoted example. Furthermore, the conference was top secret and there was a suspicion that the Ripper Gang had a mole inside the police force.

Sergeant Wilson let it be known among his colleagues that the Chief Constable's behaviour on the night of Sir Charles Grisham's arrest had been highly suspect. This little gem of speculation made its way to Zoe Porter, crime reporter at the Surrey Echo. Within a few days the Echo had made a fulsome apology for the slanderous comments in her article. However, the Home Secretary considered it prudent to be prepared for any further revelations which might surface, however unlikely, and he placed officers from Scotland Yard in charge of the case with immediate effect.

As Henry followed these developments his natural resilience and optimism returned. The Police focus now appeared to be concentrated almost entirely on catching the Ripper Gang, and the hunt for the Morderton Manor murderer had, to all intents and purposes, been kicked into the long grass. He relaxed in the knowledge that he had escaped justice and joined that exclusive band of criminals who had beaten the system and evaded capture. He was however beginning to realise that the odds against Audrey joining him were lengthening with the passage of time. She appeared to be devastated by the discovery that their savings had been transferred to an account in Spain. It was an attitude which Henry couldn't comprehend. They were moving to Spain with little possibility of returning to England. Why would you leave your assets there? He had some sympathy with her anger at being left with Mother. Henry's instruction to just hand her over to the social services had proved no easier than getting her into a private home. They had simply declined the offer. They did have nursing homes but it should come as no surprise that they all had a waiting list. Audrey faced the prospect of having to look after her husband's increasingly unpredictable and demanding mother for an indeterminable period of time while he chilled out on the Costa del Sol. The phone calls had become shorter and colder as the weeks had gone by.

His thoughts were interrupted when Harry Lee entered the bar and joined him. Harry had run a very successful business selling pop culture and comedy themed t-shirts to clubs and specialist shops in the South of England. With minimal overheads the business had been immensely profitable and he had enjoyed a lifestyle which reflected this. Unfortunately he hadn't shared his good fortune with the Inland Revenue. When he received the cumulative tax demand he realised that he would have to dispose of all his tangible assets in order to pay it. The house, the car, and the speedboat were duly sold, but Harry decided that his need was greater than that of Her Majesty's Government. He relocated to the Costa del Sol and took the money with him. He now ran a stall in Fuengirola selling t-shirts to tourists in the summer and counted Henry as one of his new best friends. About half an hour later James Mark-Turow joined them. He was born into wealthy society but without the obligatory silver spoon in his mouth. Although he hadn't inherited any wealth he had inherited the appearance of wealth and an accent which could be cut with a knife. Unwilling to prostitute himself with a normal career, he traded on his upper-class credentials shamelessly and described himself as an entrepreneur. While his many get rich quick schemes cost his investors dearly, he always stayed on the right side of the law, if sometimes dangerously close to the line. That was until he hit upon the idea of breeding grouse for shooting on a remote Scottish estate. It ticked every box for the socially aspirational clients who flocked to buy into the dream. It proved lucrative beyond his wildest imaginings. Of course it wasn't going to be lucrative if one actually built the imposing five-star lodge which graced the glossy brochure, brought the private road up to an acceptable standard, and provided grouse shooting weekends. James judged that he was unlikely to have such a ridiculously healthy bank balance again and decided that this was the time to cross the line. He retired to the Costa del Crime taking the money with him, fully aware that the fraud squad were eagerly awaiting an interview with him if he ever returned to England. He could often be found sitting outside

104

the Honolulu Bar sipping a gin and tonic, and now he too included Henry in his circle of close friends.

Their conversation turned, as it often did, to the escalating crime rate on the Costa del Sol and especially the rapid rise in burglaries. This worrying trend was universally attributed to the immigrant population, and they, like most of the expats on the coast, couldn't understand why the Spanish Government was letting people into the country who may engage in criminal activity.

It was about an hour later, while this conversation was still in full swing, that Jack Beveridge joined them. Although he was a much older man he was fit and alert, and Henry found it difficult to judge his age. Although he was not tall, he had a full head of white hair; a body which was obviously toned in the gym, and he presented an imposing figure. His piercing blue eyes only added to his commanding presence. Henry could not help but remember the video cover of the black knight which had brought him to Greywell Tunnel in search of an airborne accomplice. Smartly dressed in an expensively understated suit, the effect was spoiled for Henry by the designer trainers on his feet.

Although he knew that there must be numerous Jack Beveriges in the world, he did wonder if this might be the man who his mother had kept rambling on about. Much more reserved than the others he had met, all that he knew about him was that he had been a bank robber in the days before high-tech security made that occupation redundant, and he had the reputation for having been a bit of a ladies man in his younger days. Tonight he was in an unusually melancholic frame of mind and he had obviously been drinking before he arrived at the Honolulu Bar. The other two moved on to a livelier bar leaving Henry with a gloomy Jack Beveridge.

'They tell me you used to be a charmer with the ladies,' Henry enquired, more as a statement than a question.

Jack smiled. 'When I was a boy I had two rather large teeth which I grew into as I got older. They called me Donkey Jack at school, but it stood me in good stead when I left. The ladies

misinterpreted the nickname but I don't think I disappointed.'
He started to chuckle quietly.

'I've often wondered why no one came up with Jack Ass.
Just be thankful for small mercies I suppose.'

'How long have you been here,' Henry enquired.

'For more years than I've been in all the other places put together. I'd give my right arm to be able to fly back to Blighty and sink a pint of London Pride in the Nags Head in Tottenham. I suppose that's the downside of being a bank robber, but there are worse places to be exiled to. I'm not here because I did a few bank jobs. They only got twenty years for the Great Train Robbery and my career was much less sensational, besides which they were never able to pin a robbery on me.'

He stared into the horizon as he recalled a distant past.

'I did have my dream girl once, Bunty; but she was high maintenance,' He grinned, 'very high maintenance; and we had a son. He was a Henry. I left them for her best friend, a gorgeous leggy blonde. A gorgeous two timing bitch as it turned out. Today was the boy's birthday. I was only there for three of them. On the last one he was scared witless by a snake on late night TV. My take on a comforting hug was to tell him to pull himself together. That was therapy in those days. I often wonder what happened to him.' A smile passed his lips. 'He might have robbed a bank. Chip off the old block. The following morning I left them for the charms of a sultry blonde. I'm not here because I relieved Barclays or Lloyds of a few quid. I've never been a violent man,' he said softly, 'but I strangled that bitch. I haven't seen Spurs play at White Hart Lane in forty years or downed a decent pint of ale, and I've forgotten what a proper steak and kidney pie tastes like.' His mood changed to one of real anger.

'Dotty Henderson.' He spat the words out.

Henry was smiling broadly as he signalled the bar tender. 'Let's have another beer Jack. Do I have a story for you.'

As Henry and Jack talked over a couple of cool beers on the patio of the Honolulu Bar, back in England Mother was calling Audrey. She needed her black boots as she was going to Dotty Henderson's funeral. Well it made a change from the Pennine

Way thought Audrey as she crossed the landing and entered Mother's bedroom. If she wanted to go to a funeral, Audrey was happy to oblige. She tucked her in securely, climbed on to the bed, and sat on top of her.

She reached for the pillow.

Chapter Fourteen

Henry made a fresh cup of tea and sat down again on the balcony of his apartment. For once he was not staring contentedly out to sea. He was staring at the screen on his laptop. He had been staring at the Winkford Chronicle's weekly update on local news for over an hour. The enormity of the recent developments there was beginning to sink in. He felt some sorrow and a pang of guilt for the plight of Audrey, but his thoughts were concentrated on the possible, indeed probable, consequences that the recent turn of events was going to have on his own future. It appeared that Audrey had not as yet informed the police that her husband was the pillow case murderer. As she had been arrested over a week ago he optimistically concluded that she preferred not to divulge this information. However, whether she remained in this frame of mind would be very dependent on her future circumstances. Expediency or a desire for revenge could change her attitude at any time. It was also possible, though he felt it unlikely, that the police had been informed of his past misdemeanours by Audrey, but had chosen to withhold this information from the press for the moment.

The murder of his mother was being reported by a largely sympathetic press as a copy-cat murder by a woman under severe stress. His mother's domineering and demanding personality combined with her dementia and conversion to twenty-four hour nudism was widely reported due to various statements attributed to the Winkford W.I. Audrey was portrayed as a woman who had finally cracked up under the strain of looking after her mother-in-law while her husband, who appeared to have mental health issues of his own, was in Spain buying a bullring.

Henry had to conclude that there could be a knock on the door from the police or the press in the very near future. The fact that he wouldn't be at his mother's funeral would surely appear, at the very least, to be a bit odd.

The more pressing problem was that of his liquidity. While Audrey's coolness had presented him with a real problem, he had always felt that it was a problem he could overcome. After all Audrey was basically a very decent person who had spent the best part of her life with him. The sale of the house in Winkford was to have played a substantial part in financing their retirement in the sun. Whatever the outcome of his wife's trial, it was a real possibility that he would never see that money. The sun was shining but the future was looking bleak.

His mobile rang. The ringtone was Shirley Bassey singing 'Big Spender', which had seemed humorous when he had first arrived in Marbella in an optimistic frame of mind. He now recalled that she had also recorded, 'I who have nothing'.

It was Jack. 'Have you seen the news from home?'

He suggested that Henry move in with him until any fallout from Audrey's arrest and its possible ramifications became clearer.

'You need to disappear again while you come up with Plan B.'

Henry and Jack decided to give the Honolulu Bar a wide berth as a precautionary measure. The sun was shining and the sky was blue. The sea was undoubtedly calm but you couldn't see it from the patio outside The Fusion Bar on the outskirts of town. The 'Fusion' appeared to refer to the multicultural, if basic, menu which included tapas, pizza, pasta; kebabs, burgers, and an all day full English breakfast. Tony, the proprietor, was your stereotype Cockney and never short of a humorous response, which compensated for his unconventional grasp of customer service. If he had a colourful past it was one which he was reluctant to discuss. Henry and Jack found themselves spending ever more evenings at home, and got to know each other over Spanish beers on Jack's balcony.

Four months had passed and Henry was once more sipping his beer at the Honolulu Bar. He no longer anticipated the unwelcome knock on the door that he had been dreading. He stared at his glass and contemplated his future as he had so many times before.

'You're very quiet today,' Harry Lee quipped. 'You've been quiet for days. Don't get stressed. The police in England aren't looking for you. Mum's in her grave, Audrey's in an open prison, and the case is old news.'

Henry shot a glance at his father and then turned back to the others. After all they were his best friends now, his only friends.

'There's a cloud on the horizon. It's not imminent but it is inevitable. The money is running out and it's running out fast. I need to find a way of financing my lifestyle here.'

'Mine ran out years ago,' replied Harry. 'Why do you think I'm selling t-shirts from a stall in Fuengirola?'

James Mark-Turow turned to Henry. 'It's not easy to replenish your funds when you're effectively banished to Spain. Living the dream can become a living nightmare if you get into financial difficulties. It's a dilemma you need to resolve. I'm still solvent but I could use a decent injection of cash. It's a problem we're all going to face to some degree in the future, but not an intractable one.'

Jack smiled. 'We could rob a bank. I have some expertise and it isn't fashionable anymore.'

'I think you'll find that there's a reason for that. Bank security systems have moved on since you were in your prime and I'm not sure that they keep much cash in their vaults these days. It's all kept on their computer systems. You wouldn't want to upset the Spanish police anyway. If you upset them you'll be on the next flight to England with a one way ticket and they'll probably organise a welcoming reception for you at Heathrow.'

Jack looked thoughtful. 'We could rob a bank in England though. I reckon they still have enough cash in their vaults to make it worthwhile.'

James shook his head. 'You'd be better off robbing a currency exchange. At least you'd come away with a few euros.'

Walter Krosney spoke softly. He was an affable character with a Liverpool accent and a ready wit. He was the latest member of their little group. He'd been in Marbella for approximately six months and had joined their table just over two months ago. All they really knew about him was that he had been an antique dealer with several shops dotted around London. He appeared to have been inordinately successful and was reinventing himself as a property tycoon, if a small time property tycoon. That, and the fact that he had so readily joined their group, had led them to conclude that he had probably been a very dodgy dealer. Short and stocky with a bald head and a tattoo which left one in no doubt which football team he supported, he could have appeared quite threatening if the whole image wasn't softened by a ready smile and a cheeky glint in his eye. His interest in their life stories had caused them some concern at first, but he was now totally accepted as one of the group.

'I might be able to involve you in a nice little earner which is in the planning stage. It's a robbery, but not a bank. I'm a bit short on detail but it will happen. Henry, Harry, and James have a part to play but I'm afraid you're a bit too old Jack and your experience is not required on this one. He looked at the others. You'll solve all your money problems in one crime caper.'

'How much,' Lee asked.

'A million sterling.'

Walter Krosney smiled. He had their attention.

'A million each,' Harry enquired.

Walter looked irritated, 'You can live well in Spain with a third of a million pounds in the bank, very well, and for a very long time if you're canny with it.'

Lee was in genuine shock. 'What would we have to do?'

'It's like any business venture, the greater the risk, the greater the reward. However I have to wait until the planning process has progressed before I can give you any details.'

Henry looked uncomfortable.' Jack may be my father but he's a lot fitter than I am; a lot fitter. If he's not fit enough then I have no chance. I get breathless climbing up the hill to my apartment. A one third share of a million pounds would solve my problems but I'm not sure I'm up to it. To be more precise I'm very sure I'm not up to it.'

Walter looked at Henry and shook his head.

'That's unfortunate Henry. You see you're the one person here who is critical to the success of this venture. A million sterling, but without you it just isn't going to happen. You have a part to play Henry, and you're the only person I know who can do it. Don't be concerned by your fitness. I'm as confident in your ability to play your part as you are not. It will be a couple of weeks before I'll be able to bring you up to speed with our project. In the meantime I'll get the next round in.'

He signalled the barman and turned the conversation to the ridiculous tax on expat landlords, a subject close to his heart. The other three were staring at a bemused Henry.

When they left he promised to give them the detail, which was sadly lacking, as soon as possible and assured them that they wouldn't have to wait too long. There were time constraints on the undertaking he was proposing. He would be in touch with them shortly.

It was exactly a week later when he asked them to meet him in the Honolulu Bar at four o'clock when it would almost certainly be deserted.

Empty it was and Jack and Henry were the first to arrive. Jack opened a tab behind the bar, ordered a couple of beers, and proceeded to their table. Walter was the last to arrive. He gave a cheery wave and joined them at their table. After a few pleasantries he became serious and got down to the business of the day.

'Fate gentlemen has given us a once in a lifetime opportunity to secure our futures. I and some friends have needs and aspirations which link to yours perfectly. Like Halley's Comet this convergence of interests and events will not occur again in our lifetime. If I were a religious man I would be going to church, not to ask for God's help in transforming our financial situations, but to thank him for this opportunity which we've already been given.'

He looked round the table and saw a group of perplexed faces who were not quite sure if their latest friend was just a bit overdramatic, mentally unbalanced, or completely unhinged. As Walter turned to the bar and signalled that he wanted another beer, Lee took the opportunity to mouth the words, 'Walter

Krosney or Walter Mitty?' and he was rewarded by nods of agreement from the others.

Unaware that his audience was gaining the impression that he might be anywhere from dippy to deranged, Walter again warmed to his theme.

'Gentlemen, you have the opportunity to eradicate your individual financial problems, and in so doing you will fulfil the lifelong ambition of a business acquaintance of mine. You will also remove a problem which could potentially ruin both me and certain ex work colleagues of mine. We all play a part in achieving an outcome which requires the participation of us all and which none of us could achieve individually. There will be no second bite at this cherry. This undertaking will take place on the evening of the 25th of June, just over three months from now, and will change our lives forever.'

As yet there was no response from his audience but they were beginning to look uncomfortable. Harry was staring into his glass, James had broken his cigarette, and Henry could feel the sweat on his face. 'Walter Mitty' seemed ever more appropriate. Only Jack seemed unperturbed.

Walter continued, 'You have all trusted me with accounts of how you got here. Now I'm going to entrust you with my story, and by the end of it you will realise how much I trust you.' He paused before continuing. 'Antique dealers can make a lot of money, but not enough to buy a block of flats and several villas in Marbella. When you work in the antiques industry you come into contact with a wide mix of humanity. The generic term is dealers but they vary from the fabulously rich to life's underdogs, the impressively knowledgeable to the unscrupulous wide boys. I've dealt with them all.'

'One of my best customers over the years has been a Chinese coal magnate who is as patriotic as he is rich. He buys Chinese antiques and brings them back to China. Over the years we have built up a relationship. He has bought any authentic antiques which I have been able to acquire. I have also been able to source several very specific antiquities for his portfolio. I have always been rewarded generously. Now he sees the opportunity to acquire the one item which has always eluded him, and he is willing the pay handsomely for it.' Walter paused for effect.

'A Ming vase.'

'To put it in perspective, the last one sold at auction for £53.1 million. Unfortunately, this one isn't for sale and as it will be stolen my client would not be able to sell it again on the open market even if he wanted to. It is not an investment in the normal sense of the word. However, you will be paid one million pounds sterling for your part in its procurement, tax free, and deposited in several different banks in Spain and Portugal over a period of months to allay suspicion. Mr Junsheng will also cover any and all expenses incurred.'

He paused and looked around the table. 'The bad news is, it's going to have to be stolen from a very secure building.' He paused again for effect. He was clearly enjoying their reaction.

'The good news is. You aren't going to have to steal it.'

After another theatrical pause Walter continued.

'One day, many years ago, a young man walked into my shop in Ealing. He was well dressed in a plain but expensive sweatshirt and jeans. His shoes looked handmade and his watch was expensive. His bright blue eyes testified to his intelligence. He introduced himself, looked me in the eye, and asked me if I would consider selling stolen goods in return for a generous margin. The result of that introduction was my becoming the fifth member of a very successful gang of thieves. I became their fence. Like me they have retired. You'll have heard of them; The Ripper Gang.'

There was an audible intake of breath. Henry could feel the hairs on the back of his neck standing on end.

'We made a serious amount of money. No one outside the five of us knew of our criminal activities, not even their partners. We were very discreet and that is one of the reasons why we have evaded the long arm of the law. On top of this, Chris, the young man and gang leader, is a meticulous planner and leaves nothing to chance. The four of them are accomplished burglars and the icing on the cake, the ace up his sleeve.'

Walter paused again,

'Chris has a bent copper on his books. He refers to him as Ben T. God alone knows how that came about. He doesn't know us and only Chris knows him. However he's in too deep to be a problem and he does get very well paid for his input. If anyone could steal the Ming Vase from the British Museum it would be the Ripper Gang, but they have never committed a robbery outside a fifty mile radius of Winkford.'

Walter paused again. He looked around the table slowly.

'Prepare to be amazed.'

'Got a rabbit up your sleeve?' Harry asked.

Walter looked annoyed but ignored him and continued.

'The British Museum is taking a major exhibition celebrating the Chinese Ming Dynasty, three hundred glorious years of Chinese culture, on tour. The exhibition will include armour from that period, various artefacts, and the star of the show, a blue and white Ming Vase. The exhibition's tenth venue will be the Hayden Gallery in Winkford between Tuesday the 14th of June and Saturday the 25th. On the 25th the Ripper Gang will be among the visitors.'

Henry spoke for the first time. 'The Hayden Gallery. That's on Broadbent Square, directly opposite the police station.'

'It most certainly is.' Walter paused. 'That is where Harry and James come in. A suitably impressive distraction has been planned to occupy the police officers on duty in Winkford that evening and get them out of the town. However, Chris needs help to organise and facilitate it. Help from outside the area which cannot be traced.'

'The planning has not been a problem for Chris, but the Ripper Gang has always worked alone. They have literally no contacts who they can call on for logistical support. In this robbery their greatest asset to date is proving to be their only weakness. They have literally no connections in the criminal world. He paused again. He has looked to me to for suitable contacts but I was unable to help.'

He looked round the table.

'That is until I met James and Harry. You are intelligent and resourceful, and just as importantly, you have no connection to Winkford.'

'A robbery in England; I wouldn't be too hasty with your presumptions.' James sounded less than impressed. 'I assume any organising will be done over the internet.'

'Yes. I wouldn't jump to any conclusions,' Harry agreed. 'I think you're getting a bit ahead of yourself. And why would the Ripper Gang want to take the risk? They have retired and they are financially secure after a highly successful career.'

Henry said nothing. It was not lost on him that he no longer appeared to feature in Walter's plans and he felt a palpable sense of relief.

'It does require a trip to England. You'll have to sort that out yourselves, but if a large slice of Eastern Europe can find a way into the country it shouldn't be beyond your resourcefulness. Please just hear me out,' Walter asked.

'They have retired, are financially secure, and most importantly, Chris is extremely superstitious about doing one last job. In normal circumstances he wouldn't touch it, but we have a problem.'

'Joe Clarke, a gang member affectionately known as Shorty, has always been partial to a drink. However, he is now on a crash course to becoming an alcoholic. Furthermore, he's showing little lapses of indiscretion when he's had a skinful. It's one thing to stay at a five star hotel in Barbados for four weeks. It's another to tell the entire clientele of the George and Dragon about it. He's a plumber for God's sake, and one who's been bad mouthing the Poles for the last couple of years for forcing him to cut his hourly rate. The other three feel it necessary to babysit him when he's out and it's doing nothing for their social lives. Then there's the tattoo. It's not some small tattoo concealed on a discreet part of his body. It's a large tattoo on his upper arm and always on display. The Pink Panther to be precise, but unlike the cartoon character this one is brandishing a large lethal looking knife. It's a pictorial crossword clue for 'member of the ripper gang' and he thinks it's hilarious. But the final straw came when he bought a

116

Ferrari. It's widely believed that he's had a lottery win but he's skating on thin ice and he will take us all down with him when he goes, myself included.'

'Chris has now convinced me that the only answer is to remove him permanently, but we're not that kind of criminals. It's one thing to rob someone. It's quite another to kill someone in cold blood. Chris doesn't know anyone in that line of business and neither did I. That was until I met you Henry.'

Henry looked startled. James's eyes met Harry's and their expression spoke volumes. Walter was now confirmed as totally delusional.

So there we have it. Ling Junsheng gets the Ming vase which he has always dreamt of owning, you all get the financial security which I know you all need to varying degrees,' he said looking pointedly at Henry. 'The Ripper Gang will get the logistical support they need to pull this off, and Chris and I get rid of a potentially ruinous problem. He looked round the table. Everyone's a winner. Think it over and we'll see if it's going to happen or just be a pipe dream. But don't take too long. We're already on a tight schedule. Opportunities like this won't happen again in our lifetime. Don't spend the rest of your life regretting your decision.'

'How much do you get,' Jack asked him.

'Oh I'll get a bit more than you,' Walter replied with a smile.

'You don't appear to be taking any of the risk but you get the lion's share.'

Walter smiled. 'It's been my career to date and I can highly recommend it.'

It was Henry who broke the silence which followed. He spoke slowly and calmly. His reply was considered. His words were measured.

'I was a bit concerned at the thought of becoming a cat burglar at my time of life. I'm not as fit as I used to be and the expat lifestyle isn't helping. Getting to England without going through passport control appears to be the major problem and I for one don't know of any way around it. If that hurdle can be overcome, I feel quite confident that I will be able to solve your problem. The removal business is my area of expertise.'

As Henry looked at Harry and James he thought that he could detect a new respect in their expressions. It wasn't respect but concern; deep concern. It appeared that Walter wasn't the only person at the table who was delusional, but at least he wasn't dangerous.

Chapter Fifteen

Henry was revelling in his new persona as an international hit man. Jack was appalled.

'Don't you feel any remorse after killing someone you don't know and don't even dislike, never mind hate; any regret as they lie below you gasping for air, especially when it's a harmless old spinster?'

It was a subject which he had pointedly ignored up til now, but Henry's reaction to Walter's job offer had brought his fears of a sinister side to his son to the surface. It was more than a little disturbing.

Henry remained unperturbed. 'I didn't torture anyone. The old dears were due to meet their maker in the near future anyway. It was only a cosmic leap in medical science which was keeping them alive. Without artificial help they'd have been gasping for breath years ago. I released them from their afflictions. The only emotion I experienced was the euphoria which follows a job well done, coupled with the disappointment of not being able to share it with anyone. On this assignment the disappointment will be missing.'

Jack wasn't an expert but he had a feeling that his son was possibly a psychopath, a dangerous psychopath. One way or another he was becoming a bit creepy.

The following evening they were all back in the Honolulu Bar where Henry reiterated that he saw Walter's proposal as an answer to his pressing financial problems, if they could only find some method of entering England surreptitiously.

James shook his head in disbelief.

'Have you thought this through? Shorty Clarke may be short but he's young, probably very fit, very strong, and he sports a prominent tattoo. He's a bit different from your previous hits, two old ladies asleep in their beds, and you're not exactly the Jackal are you? You aren't fit enough to get into the boy scouts. How do you intend to kill this guy anyway? You smothered the last two with a pillow.'

Henry could feel his face going red. Furthermore he was seeing red. He glared at James and adopted the most dignified tone he could muster.

'Walter has every confidence in me and I have every confidence that I will not disappoint. Should we find our way to Winkford on the 25th of June, Shorty Clarke will breathe his last breath on that day.'

It was a show stopper. The other occupants of the table looked stunned. Jack decided it was time to bring Henry back down to earth.

'This is all hypothetical. I'm pretty sure James and Harry would be arrested the moment they arrived in England. I've a shrewd suspicion that your passports will trigger some sort of alarm at passport control, from where James will be passed on to the Fraud Squad. An interview with the Inland Revenue, which I've no doubt will prove to be extremely taxing, forgive the pun, will be convened for Harry. I don't see you just sauntering through the nothing to declare aisle unchallenged. You are probably not on any wanted list Henry, but you don't actually know what Audrey has divulged to the police, if anything. If you do get arrested they'll throw the keys away.'

Harry was finding it increasingly difficult to sympathise with Henry. He appeared to be morphing into a bit of an unsavoury character, completely at odds with the quiet, easy going friend he'd been sharing a few beers with on most nights of the week He needed a reality check.

'If you get arrested Henry you'll probably get twenty years. If there's one thing the Brits like as much as their cats and dogs it's little old ladies. That's assuming we can get to England. Walter pointed out that it's awash with illegal immigrants already, but I don't see us just jumping on the back of a lorry at Calais. Alternatively we could grease ourselves up and swim the channel. If we're successful there's the added bonus of possibly being awarded an M.B.E.'

James looked thoughtful. 'I've checked out Walter's proposal on line. The British Museum is putting a Ming Dynasty exhibition on tour and it will be at the Hayden Gallery in Winkford on the 25th of June. The star of the show is a blue and white Ming Vase described in the blurb as priceless. We know that the Ripper Gang has dropped from sight for some time now. Maybe Walter isn't as delusional as we have assumed him to be and everything he has told us is correct. Maybe we should consider his proposal. After all the Ripper Gang appear to be taking all the risks. We're taking a bigger risk than Walter but he doesn't appear to be taking any risk at all. If the robbery goes pear shaped we needn't be implicated. I can get us into England. We can just come back to Spain in the same way as we left. I have a friend, more of an acquaintance actually, who has a yacht and regularly sails across to France from his home on the south coast. A little village called Brighampton. He can pick us up and take us to his home without bothering immigration or raising any suspicions. He will do it for the same financial consideration as us. I've assured him that we'll split our million four ways and I'm sure you'll agree that it's better to earn a quarter of a million pounds than nothing at all. I have every confidence in the Ripper Gang's talent when it comes to robbery and in my ability to create the necessary diversion with Harry's help. Whether Henry succeeds or becomes the victim may be an issue for the members of the Ripper Gang, but quite frankly it doesn't affect us, other than Henry of course. This does have the potential to give us all financial security for the foreseeable future and Walter was right about one thing. We won't get this opportunity again. We know Henry is up for it, well so am I. Harry, it's down to you so no pressure, but let us know in a couple of days. We're up against the clock.'

Two days later Harry met James in the bar of the Marbella Club Hotel. James enjoyed its opulence and it seemed a suitable backdrop for a discussion on the enterprise they were considering. Harry, who hadn't crossed its threshold until now, was impressed. He needed James to allay his concerns, but he knew his decision before he entered the bar. The Winkford Ming Vase Robbery was on.

Walter was a happy man. His previously optimistic expectations of the small group of men gathered around the table of the Honolulu Bar had taken a knock at the last meeting. However, after a few days to consider his proposal rationally, they had all come round to the realisation that this was the opportunity which he already knew it to be.

Walter explained that the theft of the Ming Vase had been meticulously planned. However , because the Police Station was located across the square from the Hayden Gallery there was always the possibility, not great admittedly, but a possibility all the same, that a member of the Winkford police force would leave the Police Station at an inappropriate moment. He would see four burglars leaving a locked building which contained a priceless art collection in the middle of the night. This was the kind of scenario which Chris's meticulous planning sought to insure against. This was why a diversion had to be created of adequate proportions and geographical location to ensure that Winkford was devoid of a police presence on that evening.

'An illusionary pop concert will be advertised with non-existent tribute bands and will be located on a field eight miles out of the town. The field has been used in the past for everything from country fairs to motorbike conventions. The tickets will be cheap but the car parking spaces less so. Furthermore the spaces will be double booked and some motorists will not be allocated any specific parking place. That should guarantee that the Winkford road will be blocked solid, and the ensuing chaos should ensure that every police officer on duty that night will be out of town at the festival site.'

'Mr Junsheng has arranged for a bank account and business address to be set up in Portugal from where the concert will be organised. Gibraltar would have been preferable, but with Harry and James's interviews with the British Police and Inland Revenue outstanding, it was considered a risk not worth taking. The necessary funding had been supplied by Mr Junsheng; a minor consideration in his quest to own the Ming Vase. The whole event, even down to the hiring of staff through a Winkford employment agency, will be organised from an office in Faro. Mr Junsheng will provide you with a business phone which should only be used when organising the festival. A bank account under a false name has been opened in Tavira in Portugal, with a large initial deposit. You will be able to withdraw up to two hundred and fifty euro per day through cash dispensers. Use cash and the Portuguese debit card and make any payments to England by bank transfer. Harry and James will drive to Faro next week and get the ball rolling. Driving is a pain, but passengers on flights are easily traced. They will liaise with James's friend Terry, who has agreed to interview and employ the staff, followed by a bit of basic training, before he sets sail for Spain. It seemed prudent to be circumspect on how much we told him, so we've told him nothing of the chaos being planned. While Terry is aware that a robbery is planned, he is under the impression that the concert is a legitimate enterprise designed to get the local police out of the town in order to provide a police presence there. He'll be told about the planned diversionary chaos and the fact that the concert is going to be a non-event at a later date.'

Walter paused, 'We're on a very tight schedule now. You will have to be on hand in Winkford on the days prior to the robbery to smooth out any last minute hitches. It would be best if Henry remained away from Winkford until the day of the robbery. He is known in the town where he is thought to be to be the proprietor of a bullring here in Spain. His task is completely separate anyway.'

As Walter, James, and Harry got down to the detail, Henry and Jack drove to The Fusion Bar. Both were deep in their separate thoughts as they sipped their beers. Jack thought it prudent to keep off the subject of Henry's homicidal intention but he was worried. He finished his beer and left Henry to mull over the task which lay ahead of him. How was he going to kill a fit and strong young man? For some unfathomable reason he wanted it to be with a pillow, but that was out of the question. Stabbing was very risky, not to mention messy. The chances of him killing Shorty Clarke with a knife were very slim. A gun was the obvious weapon of choice and it would have to be a pistol which was small enough to conceal on his person, but from whom did one purchase a gun? Henry didn't mix in the right circles.

Chris Wilson had made it clear that he had a seriously bad feeling about the possible consequences of Shorty Clarke's uncontrolled tongue after robbing the Ming Vase. It would be up there with the Great Train Robbery and he would struggle to not revel in their notoriety, especially after he'd had a few too many drinks. He was a risk and Chris felt exposed. He wanted him killed straight after the robbery, and the body to just disappear. Disappear forever. It was a tall order, even for a quarter of a million pounds.

The more Henry thought about it the more certain he became that Shorty Clarke would have to be restrained while he delivered the coup de grace and dispatched him to the next world. If he was suitably restrained, he could cut his throat. Far too messy. He could strangle him. That might require a bit too much exertion. A garrotte would be easier. Alternatively, there was asphyxiation with a pillow.

Henry felt a surge of elation. It was as credible an option as any of the others, but how could he restrain an athletic young man who wasn't a willing participant. He decided that the best starting point would be to see what was on the market. Marbella's answer to Anne Summers was a shop he passed every time he drove to The Fusion Bar. It was only a couple of blocks away from it. He finished his beer and walked down the hill to Fanny's Fantasy Emporium, but as he scrutinized the tiny handcuffs encased in pink fur he knew that, however he was going to accomplish the task ahead; it was going to require something more robust than Fanny had to offer.

Henry drove home and sat on his veranda with another beer. He needed some time alone to consider how this seemingly impossible task might be accomplished and he consoled himself with the knowledge that he had faced seemingly impossible situations before and triumphed. As he pondered the problem he concluded that the intended victim would have to be totally incapacitated before he smothered him with his weapon of choice. If he was able to resist it would be a non-starter.

He considered gas; a pipe from the cars exhaust. Somehow he couldn't see Shorty Clarke just sitting in the car trying to hold his breath.

How could he get a man with a large capacity for alcohol so drunk that he was totally incapacitated, and just to make it even more implausible he would have to remain relatively sober himself.

Drugs?

Once again he moved in the wrong circles. Henry had never come into contact with drugs and had no knowledge of them. How would he obtain them? How would he know what to obtain? How would he administer them surreptitiously? He finished his beer, stifled a yawn, and decided to call it a day. He'd sleep well tonight. He smiled and the smile broadened.

Sleeping pills.

It was so obvious now that he'd thought of it. Why hadn't he thought of it before? Henry was about to become an insomniac.

Doctor Perez looked at Henry in silence for a few moments and seemed deep in thought. When he spoke his voice was slow and measured.

'You don't look much like a man who hasn't slept to me. As a matter of fact you would appear to have had a much better night's sleep than I had. My grandson' he added, as though he felt an explanation was required.

Henry left the surgery empty-handed and embarrassed. The following day he entered the surgery of Doctor Garcia, having forced himself to remain awake all night. He looked like a man who hadn't slept for over twenty-four hours, and his dishevelled appearance with dark bags under his eyes, stubble on his chin, and crumpled shirt only enhanced this view. He groaned when he saw the queue. He knew that if he surrendered to the incessant urge to close his eyes, it was highly probable that he would fall into a deep sleep in the waiting room. A night of sheer hell, which had seemed to last for an eternity, would have been for nothing.

Doctor Garcia prescribed what he described as a mild sedative. Henry explained that while he was grateful for the sedative, it was the mild which disappointed him. Could he be prescribed something a bit stronger, quite a lot stronger? When he said that he really needed a good night's sleep his voice carried conviction. However, the fact that he yawned in the middle of this request detracted from his assertion that he needed pills to accomplish it.

Doctor Garcia sat back in his chair. 'Your lack of sleep is actually not the problem,' he explained. 'It is the symptom of a problem. Very often the problem is stress and there are many causes of stress. Are you stressed Mr Hetherington-Busby? Some patients want a very strong sedative because they want a very long sleep.' He paused. 'They don't want to wake up.' He paused again. 'Ever.'

He stared at Henry, who was beginning to feel decidedly uncomfortable, but if the doctor expected any reaction from him, he was to be disappointed.

'I have never met you before Mr Hetherington-Busby. I know nothing about you. I don't know what stress, if any, may be the cause of your insomnia. I do know that I won't be prescribing you a stronger prescription than the one I have given you.'

Henry left with a prescription for a mild sedative. Doctor Garcia's final piece of advice to him was to see someone about his problem rather than the symptoms of his problem. Henry went home thoroughly dejected, flopped on to his bed, and fell into a deep sleep.

A couple of days later Henry was contemplating a third attempt to get a doctor to prescribe him some strong sleeping pills. He'd have to get it right this time. There were a limited number of surgeries in Marbella. He would need an explanation for his difficulty in sleeping which could not reasonably be attributed to stress, or any other reason which could lead one to consider a suicide attempt. He racked his brains but no flash of inspiration was forthcoming. He took a stroll into town heading for the beach and on to The Honolulu Bar, walking past a chemist's shop on route. He stopped and stared at it for a few minutes. Could it be that simple? He walked back to it and stepped inside. He approached the young girl behind the counter.

'I'm having trouble sleeping at night,' he explained. 'As a result I'm always tired and lethargic.' Henry tried to sound tired and lethargic. 'I've tried mild sedatives but they're not helping. Can you recommend anything?'

The girl nodded and gave him a knowing smile. She walked through the door into the back of the shop and returned with a box of pills in her hand. 'These would put a horse to sleep,' she informed him triumphantly, 'but they are very strong. Do not exceed the stated dose. It is dangerous, and can even be fatal.'

Henry walked to The Honolulu Bar with a spring in his step.

Chapter Sixteen

James and Harry had been in Faro for a couple of weeks but were now back in Marbella, buoyed up by their success in organising the fictitious pop concert. Finnegan's Field was booked and a suitable house rented; as were a couple of hire cars. A small employment agency in Winkford would provide the stewards for the fictitious concert. The agency had asked what training would be provided, so Harry had put together a rudimentary training course for James's friend Terry to go through with them, which he duly did. It had all been rather enjoyable. However James now advised them that his friend's yacht would be arriving off the coast in a few days time and suddenly the perilous nature of the criminal undertaking that they had embarked on was brought home to them. They could each take one small suitcase. Any extra clothing etc. which might be required would be purchased in England. Ling Junsheng had deposited funds to cover any and all expenses which might be incurred in England in the Winkford branch of Santander Bank, in the name of James Mark-Turow.

Henry had tried out one of the pills and had overslept much to his delight. They were as strong and deadly as their marketing promised. He managed to procure three more boxes of the sleeping pills by removing the pills, taking the empty box to a couple of chemist's shops, and asking for them to be replenished. It had been so easy. He crushed the pills down to a powder and now felt confident that he could wipe out the entire Ripper Gang, and then some, with his lethal cargo.

James' friend and yachtsman, Terry Levine, arrived a few days later and James brought him to the Honolulu Bar for a late lunch. He was a cheerful weather-beaten man with a nautical beard and a permanent suntan. Walter offered him some lunch and he devoured his paella with the gusto of a starving man, washing it down with several beers and no embarrassment. He clearly thought he was on an expense account and if Walter was picking up the tab, then he was happy to take full advantage of it. After an agreeable afternoon they got into their cars and followed James for a few miles down the coast to a small strip of rocky shoreline devoid of sand, and thus devoid of tourists.

'There's the Lady Carmel,' Terry said proudly, pointing to a small yacht moored close to the shore. There was total silence as they stared at the boat. It was Jack who finally said what everyone was thinking.

'When you said yacht I was expecting something bigger.'

'A lot bigger,' Henry said. 'Has it got an engine?'

'I usually sail it across the Channel to France which is twenty miles. A yacht is a boat with a sail. It isn't a description of size. It may appear small but it's a thirty footer. It's a bit of a Tardis. It will get me plus the three of you to England and back in relative comfort, and it does have an engine.'

The following morning Jack drove Henry down to the yacht as dawn was breaking. Walter was already there with James and Harry and they all sat on the rocks and had a coffee out of Terry's flask. They were dressed in jeans with t-shirts under their sweatshirts, and were carrying anoraks. Henry's clothes were mostly new as his wardrobe was predominately made up of suits or jackets and trousers. He'd only possessed one pair of jeans which Audrey had bought him for the garden and he couldn't remember when he'd felt so far out of his comfort zone. After coffee the four of them said their goodbyes to Jack and Walter, picked up their cases, and got into the small dinghy which was to ferry them to the Lady Carmel.

Jack couldn't keep the emotion from his voice as he simply said, 'be careful,' to Henry.

Henry smiled. 'I'll buy you a beer when I get back. I'll be able to afford it.'

He was the last to wade out to the dinghy and be hauled aboard. He had slipped on a seaweed covered rock and his rolled up jeans and trainers were soaking. His only consolation was that the water was warm. They boarded the yacht and went below with their cases. The boat was designed to maximise the use of the internal space. To their surprise and relief it did have sleeping accommodation for four if you utilised the sofa bed. There was a small lounge area with a table, a galley with a hob, oven, and fridge, and a small toilet which had a shower in it. Terry secured the dinghy to the bathing platform, unfurled the sail, and they headed out to sea in the stiffening breeze.

They had been at sea for about three hours before Harry started to feel queasy. An hour later he was leaning over the side as he fed the fish with the contents of his stomach. Henry turned to James,

'It's going to be a long journey.'

James just nodded. He wasn't feeling too good himself.

The sea remained relatively calm however, and the sun continued to shine. Harry just didn't seem to acclimatise to the movement of the boat and found it difficult to keep what little food he ate down. Henry had no such problem. On the third day he sat on the deck with a cup of coffee in his hand and reflected that it could be worse, a lot worse. Some people would pay handsomely for an experience like this. He hadn't been looking forward to a couple of weeks on a small boat but this was actually very pleasant. Other than a couple of ships on the horizon at any given time, they had the ocean to themselves.

'You really can disappear if you have a boat,' he said to Terry with a twinge of jealousy. 'We could go anywhere and who would know?'

'The authorities for a start,' Terry replied. 'Our boat, like all the others, is being tracked as we speak.'

'They follow our boat by satellite?' Henry sounded astounded.

'No satellites required. They use radar.' He could see the doubt on Henry's face. 'Things have moved on since the second world war you know.'

Terry pulled his mobile phone out of his pocket and pressed a few buttons. He showed Henry the screen which was a map of the Bay of Biscay with the shapes of boats on it.

'Each of those shapes represents a real boat. Let's have a look at this one.'

He touched the screen above one of the boats and its details appeared on the screen.

'Are we on it?'

'No. The Lady Carmel is quite small so I don't have to have an AIS transmitter fitted. It pin points your location very accurately and the coastguard and customs have access to it. Small boats like ours don't have to have it fitted. I do have GPS which is no different from a car's GPS but it doesn't broadcast our details to anyone else. That contraption three quarters of the way up the mast is a radar reflector. It's mandatory for us to have one fitted in European waters if we are a wooden or plastic boat, and this is how the coast guard track us with radar.'

'I thought this was supposed to be a discreet operation. Can't you take it down?'

'I could, but it might attract unnecessary suspicion if we don't have one on display. Our size will probably draw some attention to us anyway.'

'What's wrong with the size of the boat?' Henry's interest suddenly seemed keener.

'Oh, we'll be o.k. so long as we don't hit stormy weather, but the Bay of Biscay gets its fair share of storms and you wouldn't want to be sailing through one in anything smaller.'

'And then what?' Henry was no longer in idle chat mode.

'Well that's when we may all be glad that I didn't remove the radar reflector,' Terry replied with a smile.

'Not so much a clandestine operation as an exercise in health and safety.' Henry appeared to have lost his sense of humour. 'This is the first time I've been told that safety might be an issue.'

'Keep your fingers crossed.' Terry replied. He looked out to sea to hide the broad grin which lit up his face.

'Keep your fingers crossed. The last ship to sail with a similar contingency plan hit an iceberg.'

'Not much chance of that happening in the Bay of Biscay,' Terry replied calmly.

Harry and James had been listening to the conversation with mounting interest.

'This is ridiculous.' Harry whispered. He hadn't felt well since he'd boarded the Lady Carmel and they still had over a weekof sailing to look forward to. 'We could have driven to

Northern France, taken a train, or flown to Charles de Gaulle airport. I just assumed that your friend's yacht was going to be a bit more palatial. If I'd known we were going to be travelling in a floating caravan, I'd have cut the sailing time down to a minimum. The crossing from France to England could have been made in a day.'

'Well it's hardly a floating caravan but I must admit that I did think it would be bigger,' James replied defensively. 'This is the first time I've seen it and he's not so much a friend as an acquaintance. In truth I've only met him a couple of times before. I just contacted him on the off chance that he would be interested in an easy injection of cash for a minimal risk. On that point I was not wrong.'

For the rest of the trip the weather was less predictable. The calm and sunny days were broken occasionally by grey skies, angry squalls, and periods of torrential rain. A gentle sea breeze could suddenly become a ferocious headwind. While Terry assured them that these were not remotely dangerous sailing conditions, his uninitiated crew often considered the experience to be bordering on life threatening. The one odd compensation was that Harry's stomach seemed to cope with the rough seas much better than the gentle rocking motion of the calm sea.

On the thirteenth day Terry pointed out the English coastline. Although they'd followed the French coastline for some time, with England in sight the boat gave the illusion of speeding up. That evening as they turned into a small cove, they got the first glimpse of Terry's home, a large bungalow overlooking the rocky beach with what looked like a large shed or warehouse behind it. Henry had assumed that they would leave the boat in the same way as they had boarded it. However their landing on English soil was to be much more civilised. A long wooden jetty protruded out into the sea, fixed at first to large metal stakes rising from the sea bed. An extension of almost the same length was attached to it, bobbing up and down on large barrels.

Once the Lady Carmel had been securely moored they picked up their suitcases and headed for the house. A dozen or so concrete steps brought you to a gravel path which in turn brought you to the bungalow, Barton Cottage. It was a grey stone building with a dark slate roof which had the appearance of being an integral part of the surrounding countryside. A large rectangular brick building had been built directly behind it. The only other properties in view were a row of gleaming white houses with red roofs on the hillside above them. They looked deserted.

'Stanton Holiday Homes,' Terry informed them. 'They're occupied but I rarely see any of the holidaymakers. If I do, they've no real interest in me, other than to stare gormlessly at the Lady Carmel.'

They all showered, got changed, and ate pizza from the freezer. They felt their spirits lifting. Even Harry appeared to have some semblance of colour in his cheeks, although he struggled to eat his slice of pizza and steered clear of the bottled beer. It was as though he expected it to leave through the wrong orifice, even though the floor below him was not continually moving.

They rang Walter after they had settled in and left a message on his answer phone. He rang them back at eleven thirty, just as they were heading for bed. He congratulated them on the success of their journey, wished them similar success in their future endeavours, and informed them that Chris Wilson would come to Brighampton in two days time to meet them and go through the plan in detail. He had prior commitments tomorrow. The robbery was now only a week away. He was taking Shorty Clarke with him so that Henry would get a chance to appraise the intended victim.

Henry realised that he only had one day to complete a very important task. He needed to visit Audrey before he left England. He'd probably never see her again. He would somehow find a way to speak to her and offer her the chance to take a chance; to swap the misery of years of confinement for freedom in the sun.

He had checked out HM Prison Wilton Down on the internet. It was sixty miles from Winkford, a progressive institution for the rehabilitation of those who were serving a lengthy sentence, but considered to be of no risk to the community. Curtailment of liberty was the main punishment and early release was the norm. The rooms were light and airy; there was a library, a games room, and a garden that was large and landscaped. Henry had to admit it didn't look or sound too bad, but the government was unlikely to be anything other than gushing when describing one of their few innovative penal experiments. He had to give her the choice. He pulled Terry to one side and explained what he had to do and why. He had bonded with Terry more than James or Harry had, if only because he hadn't suffered seasickness. Terry agreed to drive him to Wilton Down Prison the following day without a moment's hesitation.

They set off early after a couple of slices of toast and a cup of tea. On the journey Terry was remarkably forthcoming about the road which had led him, a man who had never stolen as much as a chocolate bar, to become involved in what was clearly going to be a major crime. Henry had assumed that his past had revolved around the sea and sailing. He could not have been more mistaken. Sailing was a passion but it was a hobby. He owned a small yacht where another man might own a classic car. Terry's life revolved around apples and orchards.

Chance and changing circumstances had led him to move from the production of cooking condiments for a medium sized company where he was a quality control manager, to producing his own unique brand of balsamic vinegar. The core ingredient was apples. He teamed up with Jonathon Braun, a farmer with a large orchard and a prickly relationship with the local cider company who purchased his apples.

Terry increased the mortgage on Barton Cottage to finance the building of the production facility in his back garden and purchase the necessary equipment. It hadn't been easy. The planning application had initially been rejected and the bottling plant had to be purchased from a company in Italy. However, his perseverance eventually paid off and production commenced. As yet no supermarket had agreed to trial his product but the list of restaurants and delicatessens joining his customer base was rising steadily. After a shaky start and long hours multitasking he could see light at the end of the tunnel.

That was when Jonathon Braun felt compelled to rescue a neighbour's cat from the top of a large plum tree in his garden. The ladder fell, closely followed by the cat, as Farmer Braun grabbed a branch for support, which it failed to provide, and followed them down. The ladder was undamaged, the cat merely bounced and ran off, and Jonathon Braun died in St Mary's Hospital three days later.

The orchard had been sold to a developer for the purpose of building affordable housing. Planning permission didn't appear to have been a problem. Terry was to discover that the only apples in the area not being turned into cider were those on the local supermarket shelves.

A phone call at this point from James Mark-Turow, whom he had only met a couple of times in the past, had restored his faith in the power of prayer. James had asked him if he would be willing to bend the law a little and transport three people with slightly dodgy pasts, of whom he was one, into England for a fee of two hundred and fifty thousand pounds. He was a drowning man and he grabbed the lifeline with both hands. Several days later, when James told him that they were involved in a robbery that was being planned, he had grave misgivings, but he could see no alternative lifeline on the horizon. By the time they pulled up outside HM Prison Wilton Down, Henry felt that he knew Terry well and liked him a lot.

Henry had this idea at the back of his mind that he would spot Audrey relaxing in the garden and pop across and talk to her. The internet footage had suggested a regime so laid back and lax that he might have joined her for tea. It had not shown the intimidating entrance to the building or the high perimeter wall which surrounded what must have been the gardens that graced the website. He stared at it for about ten minutes as the realisation dawned on him that there was absolutely no chance that he would be having a conversation, however short, with Audrey. That was the point at which Terry saw the CCTV camera pointing at them and they drove into the village.

The Victoria Tea Rooms was a Mock Tudor building where the offer was cream teas, toasted sandwiches, and a selection of cakes, served by a waitress in a mock Victorian uniform. Henry and Terry each ordered the Prince Albert cream tea which consisted of the large scone with jam and cream, a choice of cake, and a pot of tea. Henry gave the waitress, whose name tag introduced her as Anne, a beaming smile and asked her if the prison visitors were good for business.

'Not just the visitors,' was her ready reply. 'It's one long holiday at that place. The inmates pop in here for afternoon tea on a regular basis, with a chaperon of course. Poor dears, I do feel for them.' No attempt was made to hide the sarcasm and Henry realised he'd touched a raw nerve.

'The Hetherington-Busby woman's in there, isn't she; the one who killed her mother–in–law.'

'Oh that one!' Anne's voice brimmed with indignation. 'She's in here once a week, laughing and joking, and she does like her cakes. Not only do I have to serve her, I'm a tax payer. I'm also paying for her cakes. The world's being turned on its head by political correctness and lily livered do-gooders. Deterrent! It's an all-inclusive holiday camp.'

Henry was more subdued on the way back to Brighampton. Audrey didn't appear to be suffering quite as much as he'd imagined. As a matter of fact she didn't seem to be suffering at all. If they could have got Mother into a place like that he'd still be an unremarkable accountant in Winkford, happily married to Audrey, and dreaming of a house on George Abbot Hill.

The following day Chris Wilson and Shorty Clarke arrived at lunchtime. The first thing Henry noticed about Shorty Clarke wasn't his tattoos which showed a partiality for cartoon characters, large breasts, and the Third Reich. It wasn't the shaven head or the earrings. It wasn't even the ring in his nose. It was his height. Shorty Clarke was six foot three. Apparently, that was why he was called Shorty.

Chapter Seventeen

Henry tried to convince himself that the fact that Shorty Clarke was getting on for a foot taller than he had expected and looked like an extra in a Mad Max movie should not concern him unduly. He would not have been unable to overpower him if he was five foot three, so the problem and its solution had not really changed. He tried to control the rising sense of panic he felt, but Shorty was not what he had anticipated. He didn't look like a nice man, and hard was not an adequate description. The solution remained the same but Henry made a mental note to double the dosage.

If Henry was shocked by Shorty Clarke's appearance, Chris Wilson was experiencing very similar emotions. James was still recovering from the voyage and was weak from the effects of two weeks in a small confined space which wouldn't keep still. Harry had never come to terms with the continual movement of the boat and the accompanying seasickness. He was pale and gaunt and his eyes had the appearance of a man desperately waiting for his therapist to turn up. However, the biggest shock was Henry, and under his calm exterior Chris was still reeling from it. Chris, like Henry, had come with certain expectations. The cold blooded killer he had envisaged was based on a couple of block buster movies he'd seen. The reality was very different. He had been expecting a Charles Bronson, but the chilling assassin who stood before him was a little fat man who wore glasses, was losing his hair, and got breathless walking to the beach and back.

They sat around the kitchen table and Chris began to go through the plan for the robbery in detail. It was at this point that Terry became aware that the concert at Finnegan's Field would not actually take place. Far from just getting Winkford's police officers out of town to provide a visible police presence and deter pickpockets, an evening of utter chaos had been planned and was anticipated. Terry's ignorance of the mayhem he had unwittingly played a part in organising did nothing to alleviate Chris's increasing concern about the competence of his new accomplices. Terry was visibly stunned, and an embarrassed 'we didn't want to worry you' from Henry didn't appear to reassure him in any way. Chris continued with his briefing. James, Harry, and now Terry, would travel with them to Winkford that evening to be trouble shooters and ensure that the diversion at Finnegan's Field went to plan with no hitches. On the day of the robbery Chris and his colleagues would enter the Museum at two thirty as the CCTV was going to suffer a glitch at two o'clock.

'Ben T is a bit of a geek which is proving invaluable on this job,' Chris explained. However, due to the forecast being that it would be the hottest day of the summer so far, they could not wear more than jeans and a t-shirt.

'It's important to be inconspicuous. This could be front page news for weeks. Shorty will be in the long sleeved variety and he'll be removing the,' he paused, 'jewellery.'

As all bags would be routinely searched they wouldn't carry anything into the building. They would make their way upstairs to the first floor, which would be deserted, at the earliest opportunity. Ben T will have concealed a length of thin rope and a weight plus a few plumbing tools required by Shorty in a cupboard. A bag has been specially designed to transport the vase. It incorporates a steel cage and it's bulky. There is no way that Ben T could smuggle it into the gallery unobtrusively. I will come back here with James, Harry, and Terry on Friday evening for a last minute briefing and we'll take Henry with us to Winkford in the morning. At four o'clock precisely we will lower the rope with the weight on the end of it from the window of the gent's toilet on the first floor. It's at the back of the building. Henry will attach the bag to it and we will haul it up.'

He saw Henry frown.

'The road at the back of the gallery is a dead end and almost always deserted, you'll have no problem parking there. Shorty will disable the staff toilets. Ben T will ensure that it displays an 'out of order' sign on the door, and that the attendant security is made aware. At that point we should not be disturbed and we can relax, but if anyone does use the toilet they won't be able to flush it, so it's unlikely that the interruption will be repeated. There are visitor's toilets downstairs anyway so there is no need for the staff ones to be used. There is also a large walk-in cupboard upstairs where we can relax during the long periods of inactivity which will make up the majority of our evening, so we shouldn't be accidentally discovered even if someone does come upstairs. Henry will return to the back of the Haydon Galley for nine o'clock when I will lower the bag with the vase in it to him. Then he can just wait in the car until Shorty joins him at eleven-twenty. You'll have a couple of hours to kill so bring a few good C.D.s or a book for company. He'll accompany you and the vase to Brighampton as security.'

He looked pointedly at Henry. He expected him to arrive there alone. Chris omitted to mention how the vase would be stolen without its disappearance being noticed. It seemed expedient not to ask.

'We will leave The Haydon Gallery at eleven twenty precisely. Security will have been reduced to a skeleton staff and Ben T will ensure that the exhibition room is empty and the doors unlocked. James and Harry can pick the rest of us up in the car park and drop us of at our respective homes before driving back to Barton Cottage. There should be total chaos on the Winkford road at Finnegan's Field and there won't be a copper for miles.'

He looked around the room with a smile.

'What could go wrong?' As an afterthought, and quite clearly not expecting a reply, he added, 'Any questions?'

It was Henry who replied.

'You will be in that gallery for quite some time. I could put a flask of coffee and four mugs in the bag. Maybe some sandwiches.'

'Now that's a really good idea,' Chris replied. 'Why didn't I think of that?'

'How do you take your coffee?'

'We're all white with two sugars, apart from Shorty who likes his black with no sugar. Always the hard man, aren't you Shorty?'

Both men smiled, but not as broadly as Henry. 'Bring me back a small flask for Shorty and a large flask for the rest of you. I'll bring coffee to the gallery, made to your individual tastes, plus sandwiches of course.'

After a short pause Terry, who still appeared to be in shock, surprised everyone by taking up the challenge.

'I'll get the flasks. Consider it done.'

Henry felt elated. He had done it again. The little fat man had confounded his critics once more. He had been dealt an appalling hand but had won the jackpot. Shorty Clarke could be seven foot three. It would make no difference. With enough sedative in his coffee to sedate a horse, asphyxiation with a pillow would be child's play.

He was and always would be the pillow killer.

Jack the Ripper hadn't shot anyone.

The Boston Strangler hadn't stabbed any of his victims.

The Barber of Seville had been a razor man. He hadn't succumbed to the temptation of a garrotting because it reduced the cleaning up to a bit of urine on the seat.

He was in illustrious company. Henry was the pillow killer, and so he would remain.

They prepared to drive to Winkford leaving Henry on his own in the house. Terry advised him to keep a low profile and ensure that the house appeared empty until they picked him up on Saturday morning. He had stocked up with provisions that morning and the freezer was full. It was advice which was unanimously agreed by all present

Before leaving Chris had managed to catch Henry on his own for a few minutes.

'A pillow,' His voice was incredulous. 'You're going to smoother him with a pillow.'

'Do you have a problem with that,' Henry asked calmly.

'I would suggest you're the one with the problem. Alongside Shorty Clarke you look like an obese Hobbit. He's an amateur boxer and a pretty good one by all accounts, and you intend to hold a pillow over his face until he snuffs it. Either this is a wind-up or you need medical help. I wasn't confident at the beginning of the conversation, and at that point I assumed you were going to shoot him.'

Now while Terry was the only person present who wasn't on Scotland Yard's, 'People we'd like to talk to' list, Henry was the only one with multiple murders on his C.V. The others couldn't come up with a single homicide between them. He felt his face turning red as the anger and resentment welled up inside him. His tone was contemptuous.

'A certain amount of tweaking will be required but you stick to the thieving and leave the grown-up bits to me.'

Chris heard the total conviction in his voice and started to doubt his previous scepticism. However, the doubts began to creep back as the car headed out of Brighampton. By the time they arrived at Winkford they were once again firmly established, and Chris Wilson was aware that he might soon be facing a very unhappy and homicidal Shorty Clarke.

Chapter Eighteen

Henry was happy to lie low in the house while the others drove to Winkford and prepared the ground for the robbery. He kept the lights off and resisted the desire to watch television. As the kitchen had a large window looking towards the rental properties on the hillside, he lived on cold meat and salad in the evenings. Boiling a kettle was his only concession to using the kitchen after the sun had gone down and he did that in the dark. He had expected to find five days in solitary increasingly difficult as time went by, but by the third day he was growing accustomed to, and actually enjoying, the solitude.

The postman called each day, dropping what appeared to be only junk mail through the letterbox. On the third day the door bell rang for several minutes before the visitor, whoever it was, went away. Henry remained quiet and hidden.

Henry considered his companions. Harry was less frosty than he had been but he was still a bit distant. Henry had brought to their attention on several occasions that if Chris thought that Shorty Clarke posed a threat to him and the rest of the Ripper Gang, then it followed that he was also a threat to them. However, Harry still seemed to have a real problem with Henry's part in their enterprise, even though it was crucial to its success in the longer term. Someone had to get their hands dirty and Henry felt that he deserved, as a minimum, their appreciation for the part he was playing. He had taken the opportunity on the voyage to point out that they were all accessories to the killing of Shorty Clarke regardless of who did the deed. Harry had got up and emptied the contents off his stomach into the ocean. This was undoubtedly due to the movement of the boat and followed a trend which had begun a few hours after sailing. However, it did seem to convey his feelings quite accurately.

James was essentially the same old James. He hadn't actually approved of Henry's enthusiasm for his undertaking, but neither had he criticised it, and Henry was happy with that.

Henry liked Terry. It was true that he was totally in the dark with regard to Henry's murderous intentions but he was an easy going companion, optimistic, cheerful, and always looking on the bright side. Everyone liked Terry.

Chris was an enigma. Intelligent and sociable, he could have been a lawyer or a stockbroker. How did he end up working and socialising with the likes of Shorty Clarke? Henry had wondered why they were robbing the gallery on the last day of the exhibition leaving no opportunity for a second attempt if they encountered an unforeseen problem. It transpired that it was because that was a day on which Ben T was on duty with a relatively inexperienced security team, plumbers were notoriously difficult to get hold of and expensive if you did, and the gallery was closed on Sunday. The planning had been well thought out with any possible complications considered, and, as far as possible, negated. He wasn't sure why Chris was so sure that the robbery wouldn't be noticed for twenty-four hours. Surely security would notice that the vase was missing within a short period of time and while the Ripper Gang were still upstairs; but on this Chris was keeping his cards very close to his chest. Henry wasn't sure if he liked Chris, but his planning appeared to be exemplary, and he did admire him.

Shorty Clarke had made a colossal impression, but it was a negative one. He encapsulated everything that Henry hated in his perceived view of the worst that humanity had to offer. While he'd never actually come into any significant contact with Societies low life, he knew that Shorty Clarke was a good representation. Henry consoled himself with the belief that he would not be missed by the rest of humanity, and would definitely not be grieved.

He considered the task in hand and felt a sense of déjà vu. Once again the devil was in the detail. He realised that the assignment which he had so recently thought would be a doddle, was actually more difficult than he had originally appreciated.

How much of the sedative should he put into Shorty's coffee? Too little and the consequences would be unthinkable. Too much and he might pass out in the gallery. Shorty's size probably meant that he would need a large dose and Henry didn't know what a normal dose was.

Then there was the unpredictability of when he drank the coffee. The earlier he drank it, the more time it would have to take effect. The best outcome would be for the drugs to incapacitate him in the car, but Henry knew that he had to err on the side of caution and make sure that he was rendered unconscious. If they did have to carry him out, at least they would be sure that there would be no police to see it. Henry had another coffee, mulled it over; and considered the dose at his leisure.

It was on Friday that it all went a bit wrong. While making a cup of coffee in the kitchen he heard a knock on the window. He looked up to see an elderly woman with a face like thunder staring at him and waving frantically. He attempted to ignore her and stared at his coffee as he added and stirred in the milk and sugar. She went round to the front door and rang the door bell.

It soon became apparent that she wasn't going to go away. Henry gave a resigned shrug, walked to the door, and opened it. She glared at him.

'Where is he?'

'He's gone away for a few days.' He presumed she must be talking about Terry.

She looked pointedly at Terry's car, parked at the side of the house.

'Where is Terry?'

She marched past him into the lounge calling 'Terry' in a loud demanding voice. Seeing that he wasn't there, she proceeded to the kitchen with Henry in hot pursuit, his protests becoming louder and more exasperated. She leant against a worktop and stared at him.

'Are you going to kill Bambi?' Her tone implied that she expected an answer.

Henry was about to reply that he wasn't about to kill anyone when some twisted sense of honour stopped him.

'Who's Bambi?'

He attempted to lighten the mood and added, 'I hope he's not a Walt Disney character or I'm several decades too late.' Her mood didn't lighten.

'It's that damned deer that's creating havoc in the allotments. It's eaten Sandra Robson's prize runner beans.' She paused for a reaction but Henry just stared at her. He was at loss for words. 'All of them,' she screamed at him. She looked exasperated.

'Where is he? He's the chairman of the allotment committee. He should have got rid of it weeks ago. The Bambi patrols are completely ineffective but they're all so bloody sentimental about the four legged vandal. It's cute. Apparently, it's cute. What's Sandra supposed to do now that it's eaten her runner beans? She had so many of them, a bumper crop. I don't know why they don't just shoot the damned thing.'

'I hope she isn't looking for compensation,' muttered Henry, unconsciously reverting to accountant mode. 'I don't think allotments are covered for accidental or any other kind of damage.'

'She'd settle for a leg of venison,' the woman snarled with real venom. 'Where is he?'Henry reiterated that he had gone away for a few days.

'And who are you?' She stared at Henry and her tone softened.' I know you.' Henry sighed. He'd been here before.

'You're that soldier from the Home Guard; the fat little captain. I thought you were dead. She stared at him. 'You look a bit different on the telly.'

Glad you noticed, thought Henry, as he informed her that makeup really does make a difference.

Henry didn't know where this conversation could lead but he did know that the woman standing in front of him was in no mood to leave quickly or quietly. He weighed up his options and concluded that the safest one was to run with a Captain Mainwaring story. Whatever yarn he was going to spin for her it would have to be pure fiction, and if it was a Dad's Army script he wouldn't trip himself up on the detail. He poured her a cup of tea and passed her the biscuit barrel as they both sat down at the table. He explained that the Christmas Special which was being planned would probably be filmed in the quiet village of Brighampton. However they didn't want a media circus to follow them about every time they visited the location.

'This has to be kept secret until they we're ready to shoot the episode,' he told her soberly. 'Otherwise another location will have to be found.'

By now they were on first name terms. She was Grace and he was Captain. He told her unequivocally that her grandson, who was apparently a trainee reporter with the local free paper, could not interview them until filming had commenced, regardless of what a boost it would be for his career. It could even put the contract with the television company in jeopardy. Henry assured her that he would get an exclusive when filming began but at as yet the t's still had to be crossed and the i's dotted. She seemed disappointed but acquiesced. She left with a bright smile and a promise to be discreet, all thoughts of Bambi purged from her mind.

The following morning Chris, James, Harry, Shorty and Terry all rose early aware that this was the big day, the culmination of months of planning. Shorty had not been on the original list but it appeared that he had enjoyed his last trip to the coast and, as Chris's Mercedes Vito had nine seats, he had invited himself along. They set off early to Brighampton to pick up Henry and take him back to Winkford. The traffic was light and they drove through Brighampton at nine fifteen. As Barton House came into view they expected to see a seemingly empty building. They didn't expect to see Henry standing in the doorway engaged in what appeared to be a highly confrontational conversation with a young man with a large camera slung over his shoulder, while an elderly woman looked on in obvious distress. They parked the car at the front of the house and surveyed the scene with real trepidation. The young man strode over to the car and Chris rolled down the window. He introduced himself as Kevin, a reporter for Avery Communications. He asked them if he could have a group photograph on the understanding that he wouldn't publish it until they gave him the nod. Chris explained that they wouldn't be posing for any picture, so it followed that there wasn't going

146

to be any requirement for a nod. He then asked him to get off what was private property. The young man didn't seem impressed and Chris became more insistent as he asked him again. Kevin ignored him and suggested that the yacht would make a perfect backdrop for the photograph. They got out of the car and, while James and Harry followed Henry into the house, Chris and Terry resumed their confrontation with their unwelcome visitors. As Terry tried to calm down the elderly woman whom he obviously knew, Shorty decided to enter the conversation, but his language was a lot more colourful. However, it was when he threatened to smash Kevin's camera, closely followed by Kevin himself, that they made their way to the woman's Nissan Micro. His tone had suggested that it wasn't an idle threat and even Terry was becoming concerned. The threats were now coming from Kevin, but they were of a legal nature and sounded more petulant than menacing. His obvious difficulty in squeezing into the passenger seat did little to add weight to his exhortations.

Had they continued to watch the car until it disappeared round the bend in the road, they would have seen the camera protruding from the car window.

Henry was still explaining the sequence of events which had led up to the morning's encounter with Grace and her grandson when they walked into the lounge. Chris looked on edge and asked them all to get into the car. This was not a good start to the big day that he had been planning for months and he wanted to get back to Winkford as soon as possible. He always appeared so calm but now he looked rattled by his skirmish with Kevin. It did nothing to diminish the uneasiness that the others were feeling to various degrees. As everyone prepared to leave, Henry asked Terry for the vacuum flasks. Terry just nodded and went out to the car. Henry switched on the kettle and took the small jar containing the sleeping powder from the cupboard. When Terry returned to the kitchen he had a large plastic bag in his hand.' I should claim for that flask on expenses,' he said with a smile. 'It's a bit bulky but it's guaranteed to keep liquid hot for twelve hours. He had also bought a large packet of chocolate biscuits. He placed the bag on the worktop. 'It might be an idea to make the coffee and sandwiches now, so that everything's ready when we get to Winkford.'

Henry nodded, looked inside at the contents, and was immediately gripped by a sense of panic. Apart from the family sized packet of biscuits there was a large thermos flask, a small carton of milk and a small packet of sugar

'Where's the small flask for Shorty's coffee?' He was aware of the tremor in his voice.

'Separate flask,' Terry chuckled. 'I can tell you're not a sailor. You've obviously never organised a picnic either. They'll add milk and sugar themselves just as you do at home or in a café.' As he walked back through the door towards the car he turned to Henry with a broad smile and added, 'you should get out more.'

Henry quickly made eight rounds of sandwiches. Dictated by the contents of the fridge it was four ham and pickle and four cheese and tomato, He put them in a bag with the biscuits. The kettle had boiled and he could hear Chris walking towards the kitchen telling him to hurry. They had to leave now.

Henry looked at the jar of sleeping powder. He'd estimated a level tablespoon would probably be about right, but he'd put in a heaped tablespoon to be on the safe side. Now there were four. Four heaped tablespoons? But they were nowhere near as big as Shorty. Three heaped tablespoons? As Chris approached the kitchen door Henry knew he had run out of time. He tipped almost half of the contents of the jar into the flask. Better too much than too little he thought, and then, for no logical reason, he tipped about half of what remained in as well and closed the lid on the jar. He added the coffee and boiling water as Chris strode into the room.

Chris watched him pour the water into the flask with a shaking hand. This was the ruthless killer who was going to suffocate Shorty Clarke later on that night with a pillow. This little fat man was to play an important part in determining the evening's outcome and Chris had played no part in the planning. He kept telling himself that Henry had done his own preparation. It was to be expected and applauded that he gave

148

nothing away. After all, he didn't look like a burglar. Walter didn't look like a fence. But he couldn't shake off a sense of foreboding. He had a bad feeling about Henry and he'd learnt to trust his instincts.

Henry packed the flask, milk, and sugar into the bag containing the sandwiches and biscuits. Chris carried it out to the car and put it into the boot alongside the padded sack which would protect the Ming Vase on its journey. He felt the same sense of elation he felt every time he set of on one of his infamous burglaries. This however was the first step in what would be the robbery of the decade. As they drove to Winkford the mood in the car was subdued, each of them lost in their own thoughts as the enormity of the endeavour ahead became a reality.

Henry's recurring thought, however, was on the task already accomplished. How did four heaped tablespoons become half a jar, and then even more? What would be the consequences?

Chapter Nineteen

Chris pulled into the car park of the Hope and Anchor pub on the outskirts of Winkford just before twelve. Shorty, who was quite obviously bored by their company, called a cab and left them while the others went inside. It was a quiet local's bar with a good, if simple, bar menu, and a selection of real ales. They sat at a corner table which was out of earshot of the other customers and went through each person's role in the day's proceedings.

As Henry tucked into his Cumberland sausages, Chris went through the forthcoming sequence of events which would culminate in James, Harry, and Terry dropping Charlie Webb, and Robert Bradbury at their homes and then driving their hired car through the night to Brighampton. Chris lived close to the town centre and would walk home. Henry would make his own way with Shorty Clarke in his hired car, arriving in Brighampton with the Ming Vase. They all stared at Henry who merely nodded and ate another mouthful of sausage, but his mind was considering the possible scenarios which now made the evening's outcome much less predictable.

The four of them might leave the gallery and fall into a deep sleep, three in their beds, and Shorty in Henry's car. He would die in a sound sleep. Very humane when you considered Sophie Delouche's final minutes, and she was a very nice person by all accounts.

If they fell asleep before they stole the vase they may well evade discovery and capture, but the robbery would have failed dramatically.

The problem would arise if they fell asleep in the gallery after stealing the vase, but before they left. The potential for them to be discovered would increase with the passage of time and, if they were still there when the robbery was discovered, they would undoubtedly wake up on the other side of the road as guests of Her Majesty's constabulary. Henry had little doubt that there would be little honour among thieves, and that they would be implicated at a very early stage in the resulting police investigation. It was all down to chance. Whether Chris Wilson, criminal mastermind and at the top of Scotland Yard's most wanted list, would succeed or fail in the most audacious criminal exploit of his career, would depend on when they had a coffee break and how much coffee they drank.

After lunch they dropped Henry off at their rented house on the outskirts of town with the sack for the vase now containing the coffee and sandwiches. They gave him the keys to his rental car, a gleaming white Vauxhall Astra, and wished him luck as they drove off. Henry stared at the sack now containing the flask of coffee. If he made a fresh flask he had enough sleeping powder to incapacitate Shorty, more than enough, but in a flask containing enough coffee for four? Henry shook his head, carried the sack into the kitchen, and left it on the worktop.

They then drove to Chris's home, a very smart detached house about a five minute walk from the Haydon Galley, left the Vito, and picked up James' hired car, a light grey Vauxhall Insignia. He drove them into town, dropped Chris in the centre, parked the car, and after a short discussion the three of them headed for Starbucks. They had a few hours to kill before heading up to Finnegan's Field. The concert was supposed to begin at seven thirty, and they had envisaged that the fans would start arriving from about six thirty, with the problems beginning sometime after seven. They would phone the police around seven fifteen, ensuring that they would arrive after seven thirty when the event should be descending into chaos. They would surely call for any available backup to be sent to their aid very quickly. This would ensure that from around eight p.m. until late into the night, other than a desk sergeant in the Broadbent Square police station, all police officers on duty would be at Finnegan's Field.

Henry drove into town at three thirty. He passed the large car park in front of the Hayden Gallery and parked in the street at the back of it. At five to four he took the sack with the coffee and sandwiches from the boot and walked up the street to the only first floor window which was ajar. The sack was heavy and he was breathless by the time he stood below the bathroom window. Chris smiled and gave him a wave as he opened the window wide and lowered the rope. A few minutes later the sack was on the first floor and Henry was driving back to the house.

It was four-thirty. Terry was becoming more and more nervous as the afternoon wore on. He had agreed to help organise the pop concert and had rather enjoyed it. It was dawning on him that he was involved in a much more serious crime than smuggling three men into the country, which was what he had originally agreed to, and one with a much more serious penalty should it lead to his being arrested. They had been in Starbucks for over three hours and he never wanted to see a coffee again. They had run out of conversation some time ago and were starting to draw the attention of the coffee shop staff. James suggested that they vacate Starbucks and drive out to the concert. It was earlier than planned, but if they got there early they could position the car for a quick and trouble-free getaway. Furthermore, he felt that an increasingly despondent Terry would benefit from being occupied. They joined the queuing traffic crawling along the road almost half a mile before the entrance to Finnegan's Field. They had intended to park just inside the entrance, but when they finally got there, this area was already full to capacity and they were forced further into the field by the convoy building up behind them. They were almost three quarters of the way up the field before Harry was able to pull off the track. He realised that he was blocking the row of cars in front of him, but more concerning were the cars which were pulling in behind him. They realised that there would be no quick exit.

Terry said that he would remain in the car as he had briefed the stewards hired for the evening over several days previously and would be instantly recognised. He didn't want to be involved when it all got out of control and now realised that his being there was a major mistake. James and Harry agreed that he had a point and should stay out of sight. They got out of the car and surveyed the scene which confronted them. They were shocked to discover that it was already teeming with unhappy gridlocked music fans. The chaos in the car park was spilling onto the area reserved for spectators, and it too was close to capacity. Some had chairs, some blankets, some picnics, and some barbecues, while the majority were just standing or milling around aimlessly. The screaming of car horns was incessant and competed with the shouting of those trying to be heard above it. James looked at his watch. It was twenty past five and already it was bedlam. They were supposed to call for police assistance at seven fifteen and drive back to Winkford. The quick getaway on which they were relying wasn't remotely possible and it dawned on him that even getting a taxi would be either problematic or impossible. They had assumed that the bulk of the concert goers would arrive much later. It was at this point that it all kicked off.

Shaun Jones was arrested and convicted for starting what the Press dubbed 'The Winkford Road Rage Riot'. To this day he remains aggrieved at being singled out as the ringleader in the mayhem which descended on Finnegan's Field that afternoon. When he entered Finnegan's Field ten minutes earlier he had been queuing for over half an hour. This had followed a three hour drive with a sullen wife and three argumentative teenagers, and he was seriously stressed. He entered an area of seething anger and resentment where the violence simmering beneath the surface was palpable. He had paid for a specific parking spot which already had a car parked in it. The area of the field which was designated as the car park was full and spreading on to the waste ground which bordered it. The argument which ensued was being replicated by dozens of other exasperated drivers, convinced that the parking spaces they had paid for had been stolen.

Shaun's claim to fame was that he was the man who lost control before any of the others. However, it was as though they had all been waiting for a signal. When Shaun punched the driver of the car who had parked in his allotted space and insisted it was actually his, they collectively embraced it as the sign they had been waiting for. Within a few minutes the area around Shaun was ugly, deteriorating by the minute, and spreading through the car park like wildfire. The police on duty who had expected a few hours of easy overtime called for

153

reinforcements urgently. When they eventually managed to reach the festival site, the officer in charge rang Chief Superintendent Donovan directly, describing the scene which confronted him as a riot the likes of which had not been seen in England for decades.

By six-thirty the Home Secretary had been informed and the adjoining police forces of Hampshire, Berkshire, and Middlesex, were sending reinforcements to Winkford. The police station was considered too small, so a control centre was set up in the large entrance hall of the Haydon Gallery across the street.

Henry was sitting in the lounge watching the television with the alarm clock sitting on the coffee table and set for eight-thirty. He was blissfully unaware of the drama unfolding in the town. At ten past seven his mobile phone rang. It was Harry who informed him that they'd hit a bit of a problem and couldn't get the car out of the car park. Could he pick him and Terry up on the road? James would stay with the car. They were making their way back to Winkford as he spoke. Henry was perplexed but Harry didn't seem to want to go into detail so he obliged. He was actually quite happy to have something constructive to do. He'd been unable to concentrate on the television and had eventually turned it off, passing the time by drinking tea and continually glancing at the clock. It was with a sense of relief that he locked the door behind him and got back into his car. As he drove into the centre of town he was overtaken by two police vans, both full of police officers. Broadbent Square was a hive of activity and half a mile beyond it there was a police road block stopping cars from taking the road out of town in the direction of Finnegan's Field. The alternative route, leaving the town in the opposite direction, was also blocked at its junction with Winkford road. Vehicles were being allowed into the town but not out of it. Henry assumed that the road to Finnegan's Field would be blocked to vehicles coming from the opposite direction as well. The police may not have quelled all the violence on the festival site as yet but they certainly had the problem contained. He decided to drive to the gallery and park at the back. As he drove round the square another fully loaded police van was pulling into the car park in front of it. The square was beginning to attract a crowd of mainly young men and women who sensed that this Saturday night might be more eventful than most in sleepy Winkford. The police were trying to move them on but only half-heartedly. The last thing they needed was trouble in the town centre. He drove up the side of the gallery, round the back, and was relieved to find one parking space free. There had never been a problem with parking before. The massive police presence was obviously pulling spectators into the town as the word got out. They hadn't foreseen that. He wondered what else hadn't been foreseen. He phoned Harry and explained that neither he nor a taxi, nor anyone else would be picking them up.

However that wasn't the bad news.

'What do you mean' Harry sounded worried. He was. What else was going tits up he thought? Henry's voice became dramatic to compliment the gravity of the situation.

'They've been caught. It's all over, and that Ming Vase is highly valued in some very influential circles. The sooner we disappear back to Spain the better.'

'How do you know?'

'Hayden's Gallery is swarming with police and Broadbent Square resembles a police academy on Graduation Day. How's that for a clue? I doubt there's been so many police in one place since the miners' strike.'

Harry explained the situation at Finnegan's Field.

'So they may not have been caught,' Henry conceded 'but it's only a matter of time.'

Harry considered the situation before replying.

'They just have to keep their nerve and wait until the trouble at the field is sorted, and it's already a lot calmer judging by the reduction in noise coming from it. The Ripper Gang are not noted for losing their nerve so I think we can be reasonably confident that they'll just walk out sometime tomorrow when the excitement is over. In the meantime just collect the vase as planned.'

They decided that they just couldn't take the risk of Terry being recognised by any of the festival staff, so he continued walking back towards Winkford while Harry made his way back to the car and brought James up to date with the latest developments.

Henry sat in his car and turned on the radio. He adjusted his seat to a more relaxing position and wondered how much coffee was being consumed on the first floor of the gallery as he waited for nine o'clock. He tuned into the local radio channel and waited for the news. When it came it dwelt on the success of the Chinese Ming Period Exhibition but no mention was made of any problems at the Finnegan's Field concert. However, a traffic update ten minutes later informed the listeners that due to an incident at the concert the road to it had been closed at Winkford on one side and Byfleet on the other. No details were given and one would have assumed it was a traffic incident if you didn't have inside information. Panic management, Henry concluded.

The road at the back of the gallery remained deserted apart from the occasional car looking for a parking space and leaving on being disappointed. The eight thirty news bulletin reported that the incident at Finnegan's Field had required a significant police presence but that the situation, while ongoing, was now under control. Further information would follow as it became available. The traffic updates would remain unchanged for several hours.

At nine o'clock Henry left the car, walked down the road, and looked up at the first floor bathroom window. Chris was looking out and gave him the thumbs up. He felt a palpable surge of relief. So far so good he thought. The window opened and the sack containing the vase was lowered down to him. He untied it and returned the thumbs up. Chris's response was to rub his eyes and give an almighty yawn. They weren't due to leave the building for over two hours.

Henry reassessed his 'so far so good' as he put the sack containing the vase into the boot and got back into the car to await developments. It only now dawned on him that Chris and the rest of his gang might be blissfully unaware of the massive

156

police presence in Winkford town centre. He assumed that 'Ben T' would have updated them but he no longer took anything for granted. He tried ringing Chris on his mobile but it was switched off. Assuming that they knew, it was surely out of the question for them to leave the building at twenty past eleven as planned now that the entrance hall had been turned into a police control centre. One could only hope that they would fall asleep and remain undetected until they woke up when the crisis and the police had dispersed. Would the evening conclude with a triumph or a catastrophe? The odds on a triumph were beginning to lengthen. When the twelve o'clock news came on, Henry turned off the radio and phoned Harry. He updated him with the fact that there had been no sign of Shorty and the other gang members. They were obviously trapped in the gallery by the police presence. He was going to drive back to the house. He saw no benefit in telling him that they could be in a deep sleep as they spoke.

James and Harry were sitting in their car watching events unfolding around them when they received Henry's call. The police now occupied the field in strength and order, if not calm, had been restored. Removing the vehicles from the field was proving painfully slow and they anticipated it being a long night. They assumed that the Ripper Gang would also be having a long night waiting for the police to disperse from the building.

'Just as well Henry thought of the coffee and sandwiches,' Harry remarked.

Henry adjusted his seat, started the engine, and headed back to the house. There were now only a couple of police vans in the car park and about a dozen police officers smoking and generally milling about outside the gallery. He presumed the rest were at the festival site. He drove through the town slowly, staying scrupulously within the speed limit, and put the kettle on when he got home. He was tired, but he felt the same need to stay up that he always felt on election night.

Harry and James didn't get out of the field until ten to one and made their way back to Winkford. They rang Terry to tell him that they were on their way but he didn't answer his phone.

'Must have run out of power,' Harry said, but his voice lacked conviction and James didn't look convinced either.

The traffic speed had picked up and they were in a giant convoy. They scanned the darkness on the side of the road for Terry walking back towards Winkford but as they approached the town there was no sign of him.

'What's he playing at?' James asked. It was a rhetorical question.

They drove through Broadbent Square just as two stretchers were being loaded onto one of the two ambulances parked outside the Haydon Gallery.

'Maybe Shorty died resisting arrest,' Harry suggested.

'Let's hope one of the others died with him and the second stretcher isn't a policeman,' James replied, 'and let's hope the second ambulance is a precautionary measure.' He gave a long sigh. 'What have we got ourselves into?'

When they got back to the house at ten to two Henry was sitting in front of the television awaiting their arrival and they updated him on the latest situation over a cup of coffee. Things didn't look good for the Ripper Gang and Terry had disappeared. It was Henry who brought an optimistic note into the conversation. While not divulging the part that his coffee might have played in the evening's events, he did point out that they did have possession of the Ming Vase and that provided Terry got in contact in the very near future all was not lost. They didn't need the Ripper Gang, but they did need Terry.

'In layman's terms, we need someone to drive the boat.'

They were by now beyond tiredness and Henry made three fresh mugs of coffee as they awaited developments, or to be more precise, the arrival of Terry. They didn't have long to wait. About twenty minutes later they heard a car turn into the drive. All three of them walked quickly to the door and Harry opened it. A police car was pulling up outside and they could see a distraught and dishevelled Terry sitting in the back seat.

Chapter Twenty

When Harry returned to the car James had fully understood why Terry had decided to keep walking to Winkford, and agreed with his reasoning. They had done all the planning from Portugal while Terry had dealt with the face to face coordination of the event. They had organised the fantasy festival by phone and email while Terry was their man at the sharp end, smoothing out any problems and allaying the concerns of the troops on the ground as and when they arose. It had seemed a sensible division of labour at the time but now they wondered if Terry had possibly been a bit naive. While they were faceless entities at the end of a phone or computer terminal, he had spent time with the agents, attended meetings with the advertisers, and spent an evening in the pub with the stewards who were now experiencing levels of stress which they could never have dreamt of. It was only rational for Terry to put as many miles as humanly possible between himself and the festival site as quickly as possible. He had been lucky to leave unobserved. Returning to the site was out of the question.

Terry had watched Harry walk round the bend in the road and out of sight before he set of in the direction of Winkford. He walked quickly, and was only marginally slower than the traffic crawling in the same direction as he stuck his thumb out more in hope than expectation. If he thought someone might take pity on him, he was to be disappointed. The tired and angry mass of humanity that slowly passed him was in no mood to produce a Good Samaritan. After walking for about an hour, he came across a large tree stump at the side of the road. He was tired and hungry and could see no point in walking any further. Eventually, James and Harry would get out of the festival car park, stop to pick him up, and take him back to Winkford. He sat on it and after about twenty minutes felt the need to get more comfortable and lay against it. About ten minutes later he lay alongside it, and that was when he succumbed to the overwhelming desire to shut his eyes and sleep.

At about one o'clock the peace and calm which had descended on the previously hectic Haydon Gallery was abruptly shattered. WPC Johnson had been sent upstairs to find a whiteboard where she found four men apparently sleeping in a small room used for storage. She attempted to wake one of them up without success and moved on to a second. This led to the morbid discovery which was relayed to her colleagues downstairs by her hysterical screaming. WPC Johnson had been exemplary on her training course, but she had only passed out of college six months previously. Her career to date had been a combination of talking to school children on the dangers of drugs and binge drinking, and patrolling the safe and uneventful streets of Winkford. It had not prepared her for finding dead bodies in the police control centre.

Frankly, none of the police present were prepared for such a discovery. All four men were dead and they had no idea who they were or what they were doing there. There was no sign of foul play. Were they employees? Why were they in the storage cupboard? As they waited for two ambulances to be diverted from Finnegan's Field an impromptu brainstorming session got under way in the Haydon Gallery. Brainstorming sessions can lead to some very random possibilities. Was there a gas leak? Could it be the result of an academic power struggle? Was it a mass suicide? To Constable Herriot who had spent his working life patrolling the sleepy villages and small country towns around Winkford, and was destined to retire as a police constable, the possibility of witchcraft and sorcery was a line of enquiry not to be discarded lightly. It was a theory which led to equal measures of incredulity and hilarity as it spread rapidly throughout the assembled police forces in the square. The probability of a robbery gone wrong was beginning to gain credence, but the lethal intervention of some supernatural force remained a much discussed, if light-hearted, option.

Terry was now awake again and was sitting on the tree stump as he scoured the traffic, which had speeded up noticeably, for James and Harry. He saw the two ambulances heading for Winkford at speed on the wrong side of the road, and with a police escort. Given that the trouble appeared to be over this did seem a bit strange, but no stranger than the rest of the evening so he didn't dwell on it. It could be a random birth or heart attack he thought, but two ambulances? It could be both. A birth, a heart attack! It could be a stroke, an asthma attack, a broken arm or leg. The ambulances suddenly seemed unimportant and he purged them from his mind as he rang James for an update on their situation.

James, whom he had never heard lose his composure before, told him to stay put as, 'we expect to get out of this flaming field eventually,' and on that note ended the conversation.

Suddenly, against all his expectations an old Ford Zephyr, its blue paint faded, slowed down and pulled up a hundred yards ahead of him. He wasn't convinced that James's and Harry's arrival would be imminent and his heart leapt as he trotted towards the stationary car. He stopped abruptly when a passenger opened the back door and got out. He recognised him immediately as Peter, one of the festival stewards.

'Oiy, you,' the young man bellowed. 'We want a word with you.'

He sounded upset, very upset, as he started to run towards Terry. A second steward was now getting out of the passenger seat. The young man racing towards him didn't look as though he wanted a calm and considered discussion on the evening's developments. Terry made a spontaneous decision. This wasn't the time for any kind of discussion. He climbed over the fence, jumped into the field which bordered the road, and ran towards the trees on the far side as fast as his legs would carry him. The clump of woodland seemed a long way off but it offered the best chance of evading his pursuer. Although he was twice the age of the young man chasing him, Terry maintained the distance between them. This was partly because he was physically fit and partly due to the sense of fear which was gripping him. For the first time the hint of danger that accompanied their exploits had become a reality. With the trees tantalisingly close, the ground became increasingly soft. He slipped at speed, was winded and covered in mud. By the time he had recovered and got to his feet his pursuer was just behind him. A few yards later he experienced a near perfect rugby tackle and they both hit the ground together. Terry knew that Peter, his assailant, was a quiet young man with a mild learning disability. He felt his head being yanked up by his hair and then being smashed into the mud, again, and again and then again. He obviously had a darker side, and ominously, one which had surfaced tonight.

'What happened to the concert?'

He sounded demonic and Terry felt shell-shocked. He was rapidly progressing from being seriously concerned to being absolutely terrified. When the punch landed on his cheek he realised that Peter wasn't just psychotic, he was positively certifiable.

'What happened to the concert? What happened?'

At this point Derek, who was known as Chas for some inexplicable reason, turned up. Any faint hope that he might be a restraining influence was quickly dispelled when Chas kicked him viciously in the leg.

'He asked you a question.' Chas was calm, almost polite, and actually the scarier of the two. Terry's brain slipped into gear.

'The police stopped it. They cancelled it at the first sign of trouble. They closed the road and turned the bands away.' His audience seemed to be listening, and more importantly, calming down.

Terry warmed to his theme. It was having the desired effect. Peter let go of his hair and unclenched the fist which was threatening him.

'I was escorted off the site, on foot, not even driven back to Winkford. I've ploughed every penny I had into this concert and borrowed to the hilt. I'm ruined.'

His two assailants seemed satisfied, even rather pleased by his financial predicament. Peter got off his back and Chas stamped on his left hand with the heel of his boot, before they both walked across the field towards their car.

Terry sat in the mud for about fifteen minutes. He fought back the frequent desire to burst into tears but he felt himself slowly descending into a pit of depression. Nothing he had ever experienced had prepared him for this. He had braved the elements in mountainous seas, had faced bankruptcy and ruin with a stoic dignity, but nothing had equipped him to cope with the situation he found himself in now, and he had a horrific premonition that this was the tip of the iceberg. A simple, if illegal, resolution to an intractable financial dilemma had led him into a murky world of lawlessness and danger; a world he had previously only associated with the fantasies of the silver screen. His head hurt, his leg ached, his left hand throbbed agonizingly, and his throat was dry, but none of that compared with the pit in his stomach as he searched in his pockets for his mobile phone. He got to his knees and probed the long grass and mud around him in the gloom. He stood up and headed slowly back towards the road. It looked like he might be walking to Winkford after all.

He had only been walking along the road for about twenty minutes when a police car pulled up alongside him. The officer in the passenger seat asked him if he was OK. His voice left no doubt that he didn't believe this to be the case. Terry went along with their supposition that his sorry state had resulted from a confrontation at the festival site. Any complaint against the real attackers was out of the question. He was helped into the back seat and the car headed off towards Winkford. The policeman in the passenger seat sounded genuinely concerned.

'What happened to you then?' he enquired.

He saw that Terry was cradling his left hand in his right one and that the left one was grotesquely swollen and bruised.

'We better get you to hospital. That hand of yours needs looking at.'

Terry tended to agree but he grimaced and told him that it would be alright. He had a feeling that a visit to a hospital might lead to difficult questions from people with good memories and equally good descriptive powers.

'Just drop me off at a taxi rank in town and I'll make my way home from there. You look like you've had a busy night yourselves.'

'Oh we can do better than that,' the policeman replied. 'Where do you live?'

Terry was tired, physically exhausted, and his hand was throbbing painfully. He was caked in mud and very aware that he was riding in a police car while probably being one of the most wanted men in Winkford. Now they wanted to know where he lived. He broke into a cold sweat as he willed a suitable response to come to mind, anything which would enable him to conceal his address. His mind remained stubbornly blank. After a short pause he thanked them profusely and gave them his address. As they passed through Broadbent Square they saw an ambulance parking alongside the Haydon Gallery and there was an ominous silence among the police milling around the gallery entrance. The police car pulled into the side and the driver opened his window.

'What's happening,' he asked a policeman standing on the pavement.

'Well, that's the question we're all asking,' he replied gravely. 'The Control Centre turned out to be some sort of temporary morgue with four dead bodies hidden in the cupboards. They've been moved to the official morgue. Apparently the local constabulary think that either the hags from the Winkford witches coven have been out on a bender, or the local vampires have been taking advantage of the heavy cloud cover and having an orgy. They've sent us another ambulance. Presumably that's in case we find any more corpses secreted around the building. No sign of punctures to the neck but they're taking no chances,' he added. 'They've put out an APB for a pale man in a black cloak, sporting a couple of fangs, and flying around the town.' He was obviously aware of the supernatural intervention theories of Constable Herriot and was singularly unimpressed. He warmed to his theme.

'They're trying to locate the manager of the local Tesco so that we can arm ourselves with garlic and the S.W.A.T team are waiting for a supply of silver bullets.'

'You can't be too careful.' His tone became sombre. 'Truth is, there's been more violence in the Control Centre than at the Festival but nobody heard a thing. Who'd want to live in the country? It's positively creepy if you ask me. At least you know where you are with the mindless thugs who saunter through our city streets, especially now that we can appreciate the influences of their formative years, their environment, and not forgetting their anger management problems.'

The two policemen in the car looked at each other without speaking. He'd obviously been on a course. He clearly hadn't been receptive to the message. They wished him luck and drove on. Terry felt any sense of optimism ebbing away as he dwelt again on this parallel universe which he had entered, where extreme violence appeared to be the norm and personal safety was not to be taken for granted. They pulled into the driveway of the rented house and the expression on Harry's face as he opened the door did nothing to ease his concerns.

Terry's arrival had signalled the end of the evening. Suddenly, everyone felt numbingly tired. James joined Harry in thanking the two police officers profusely before following Terry and Henry into the kitchen. Terry gave them the bare bones of his story over a coffee and told them that all four members of the Ripper Gang were apparently dead. This was an outcome that no one other than Henry had even considered. It was bizarre. Henry considered it prudent to keep his part in their demise to himself for now. When James concluded that 'it will all come out in the wash,' they all nodded in agreement and headed to bed exhausted.

Chapter Twenty-One

Surprisingly, they were all back in the kitchen for breakfast by ten o'clock the following morning. A subdued Terry gave the full version of his ill-fated previous evening over a poached egg on toast. He appeared to have been disproportionately affected by his experiences and seemed over anxious about the potential consequences of their criminal actions. He had a premonition that the violence of the previous evening was likely to occur again in the near future. His assertion that the vase was cursed was greeted with derision until they realised just how serious he was. He felt that he was in a storm, one that he was ill-prepared to weather, and that they were all in deadly peril. He was cracking up in front of them and they were at a loss how to deal with it.

It was Henry who steered the conversation into calmer waters. In the early morning, while the others had still been sleeping, he had given a great deal of thought to their present position, and his conclusions were reassuring. He pointed out that there was no tangible connection between themselves and the Ripper Gang other than possibly Barton Cottage; a link so tenuous that he was confident it would never surface. He looked thoughtful as he continued.

'The most puzzling thing is that no one seems to have noticed that the Ming Vase is missing. The one unfathomable part of the robbery was how the theft of the vase would not be noticed between the time that it was stolen and the time that the gang would escape from the building hours later. It still hasn't been reported as missing even though four dead bodies have been found in the building, and that is baffling; quite inexplicable. Chris had been tight lipped on this part of his plan and we all assumed that it was in some way linked to his police accomplice. With the benefit of hindsight, it now seems inconceivable to me that one police officer could somehow hide the theft of the centrepiece of the exhibition from his colleagues for several hours. I can only conclude that it isn't missing and it was never going to be missing.' He had their attention.

'But it's in the boot of your car,' Harry said. 'We know it is.'

'A vase is in the back of our car. Of that I have no doubt. Is it the Ming Vase? I very much doubt it. Chris didn't undertake this robbery for the money. No one in the Ripper Gang needs money. He didn't do it for the kudos. Their success up til now can be largely attributed to their anonymity which he intended to take to the grave. He had a superstitious fear that this would be the one which would go wrong, their last job. So why did he agree to it? What he really wanted was to rid himself of the problem that an increasingly unpredictable Shorty Clarke had become. We all wondered why he was so sure that the theft of the vase wouldn't be discovered while they were still in the building, and it was the one detail on which he was unwilling to illuminate us. He knew that the disappearance of the vase wouldn't be discovered because it hasn't disappeared. It's still there. They would not be caught executing their last robbery because there was to be no robbery. However, the Shorty Clarke problem would be laid to rest, quite literally. So we aren't going to become millionaires, but neither will we become guests of Her Majesty. There is nothing which will link us to the Ripper Gang as far as I am aware. We can all go home and work out some other way of financing our retirement in the certain knowledge that if something seems too good to be true, it probably is.'

'I hope Walter and Mr Junsheng don't think we've double-crossed them.' Terry's voice oozed depression. 'I could see our situation deteriorating rapidly if that were the case.'

'There's no chance of that happening,' Henry replied emphatically. 'The real Ming Vase is still on display in the Haydon Gallery for the world to see. However, if we bring back the vase which is in the boot of my car, it is possible that we might receive a payment for our trouble. Mr Junsheng is, according to Walter, a very wealthy man and an honourable one.'

167

The journey to Barton Cottage was made in silence for the most part. Their minds were occupied by their own thoughts. Terry's thoughts appeared to be so dark that they didn't want to tap into them. Quite why he appeared so downcast was a bit of a mystery. His despondency didn't reflect their actual situation which, given the course of events on the previous day, could have been considerably worse. He looked close to tears. Henry's attempts to cheer him up only seemed to add to his gloom and he gave up trying to pull him out of the pit of despair that he appeared to be sinking into. It proved to be the right decision and as the journey neared its end he seemed to have recovered somewhat, although he remained withdrawn. The others all now considered him to be the weak link in their group and Henry saw him as a real cause for concern. Any sign of a light at the end of Terry's dark tunnel was viewed with some relief. There was further relief when Barton Cottage came into view. The nightmare that would forever be associated with Winkford seemed finally to be in the past. Tomorrow they would consider the future. The events of the last few weeks would have to be scrutinised and any loose ends would have to be tied up. The inevitable police investigation would have to find no link with Barton Cottage. The hired cars and Terry's missing phone were the only problems that came to mind initially. One car was parked in Winkford but the other was now parked outside the cottage and they no longer had Chris to drive it back there. James was volunteered to drive it to the outskirts of London the following day, park it near a railway station, and get a train back to Brighampton. He would then drive to Winkford with Terry in the next few days and attempt to locate his phone and SIM card. Once the loose ends had been tied up, the trip back to Spain would be the final chapter in the whole sorry enterprise. After supper, which consisted of a full English breakfast followed by an early night, they all woke fresh and reinvigorated in the morning. Even Terry was able to crack a smile.

Henry picked up the free paper which was delivered at around nine o'clock. He threw it onto the dining table where it remained until Terry picked it up around eleven as they all sat down to Harry's brunch, another cooked breakfast. The picture which filled the top half of page three was of Terry, Shorty, and Chris Wilson outside Barton Cottage. Shorty was heading into the cottage and his face was obscured, but a large tattoo of the Pink Panther wielding a knife was clearly visible on his upper arm. The short article alongside it was headed, 'Dad's Army Comes To Brighamton.'

'You better have a look at this', he said gravely as he passed the paper to Henry. As he stared at the article in front of him Henry did something totally out of character. He swore. Harry and James immediately came across to view the cause of his concern. Harry also swore but this was not out of character, while James merely shook his head in disbelief.

Henry summed up their situation. 'Barton Cottage is now linked to the Ripper Gang and that's a bit unfortunate. The members of the Ripper Gang will be identified in the very near future and it is inconceivable that Shorty's tattoo won't be mentioned in any of the ensuing news items of which I have no doubt there will be many.'

As the owner of Barton Cottage and in the picture with a member of the Ripper Gang, you Terry, are very definitely linked with the events in Winkford to some extent. A character bearing an uncanny resemblance to Captain Mainwaring is also linked to those events due to his presence in the cottage being discovered by an overbearing old aunt and her nephew, the reporter who took the photograph. However, I am quite confident that investigations into his whereabouts will not lead to me. A Captain Mainwaring look-alike is already on the Winkford police most wanted list and I am, after all, officially residing in Spain as we speak. There are a lot of Captain Mainwaring impersonators out there,' he added with a broad grin as he remembered the hilarious news story of the police lineup in Winkford police station. 'Sir Charles Grisham on the other hand may receive a knock on the door in the very near future. Harry and James were only seen at the cottage for a very short period of time and their descriptions will be so vague as to be useless. They were also seen by the two police officers, who drove Terry home from the festival, but it was a fleeting sighting in the dark and any description will be equally useless.'

He turned to Terry and any optimism drained from his voice.

'I wish I could say the same for you Terry. You trained, for want of a better word, the festival staff. You got so close to them that they wanted to beat you up when the festival fell apart and will be able to give a highly accurate description of you. You drove home, not in our car as planned, as you were running for your life through a muddy field when we passed by. Not in a taxi, because you needed a phone to contact a taxi and yours is lying in a muddy field at present, waiting to be found; and with all our phone numbers on it. No, you hitched a ride home with a couple of police officers. However, it just so happens that they, like your festival fans, will not have to rely on their memory to give a detailed description of you because your photograph is alongside that of Chris and Shorty Clarke in today's issue of the Brighampton Gazette. Several of its readers are going to remember where they saw that tattoo when photographs of the Ripper Gang are published in the national press. If they don't, the young reporter who took the photograph and most of the editorial staff at the Gazette definitely will. Barton Cottage is going to receive a visit from Scotland Yard in the very near future and we better not be here.'

Chapter Twenty-Two

The discussion that followed led to a couple of conclusions quite quickly. The first was that all was not lost if they reacted with speed, but they had little time, maybe as little as twenty-four hours. Harry and a shell-shocked Terry would drive that morning to Winkford in Terry's car and the hired car. They would park the hired car in Winkford, locate and retrieve the mobile phone, and return to Brighampton in Terry's car. That would tie up all the loose ends, bar Terry. He was more than a loose end; he was the torpedo who could sink them. James would stay at Barton Cottage and help Henry clean it of any evidence which could be linked to them. This included the cleaning of all areas they had occupied and the wearing of rubber gloves from this point onwards. Terry had only one option it would appear, to clear his bank accounts of as much money as he could and join them in their brave new world, the Costa Del Crime. Terry was appalled but could think of no alternative. He was becoming close to suicidal, and Henry couldn't help but think that this would be the most helpful thing he could do. The trouble was that he was the only sailor among them. Without Terry they wouldn't be able to sail out of the harbour, never mind to France. Terry had to be kept very much alive.

The mission to Winkford was as successful as it was uneventful. Finding the phone had always seemed a touch optimistic but in reality they had found it remarkably quickly in daylight. They returned shortly after seven but Terry seemed unaffected by the sense of optimism which now pervaded the group. After a quick meal of sausage and mash washed down with a few bottles of beer, they cleared the dishes from the kitchen table and sat down to consider their next move. There was a sense of urgency and a realisation that they had to act quickly. The link between Shorty Clarke and Barton Cottage would be made. That seemed inevitable once the description of his unique tattoo reached the press. The Brighampton Gazette's readership could be ringing the local constabulary within hours, and this would be quickly followed by a visit to Barton Cottage by Surrey C.I.D. or Scotland Yard.

They concluded that sailing to France was the obvious course of action from where Jack could collect them and take them overland to Marbella. Henry told Terry that he could remain holed up in his apartment until 'things' had settled down to a point where he could 'move on'. Terry was appreciative to the point of tears while James and Harry looked positively shocked. Terry promised them that whatever the future held, he would not 'drop them in it' and Henry appeared quite happy with this assurance. They phoned Jack who was delighted to hear from them, and assured them that he could collect them on Tuesday evening. On being brought up to date on Terry's situation he pointed out that if he was traced to Henry's apartment, Henry's likeness to Captain Mainwaring would probably not go unnoticed, but Henry appeared remarkably unconcerned. They would leave the day after tomorrow. Terry, whose future seemed bleak whatever happened, seemed unconvinced by the plan, but James was equally sceptical. He considered the idea of a high profile wanted criminal, one who could be linked to them, moving in with Henry, to be bordering on lunacy. He came up with an alternative plan a couple of hours later. He suggested that they change the name of the boat. Terry could just sail into the sunset until he found a picturesque watering hole where he could continue his life with a clean sheet. Terry revealed that he did know of an identical boat that was moored in Poole Marina. He knew the elderly owner and that it rarely ventured from its mooring. While he couldn't be described as happy he did now have a Plan B of sorts. After raising as much cash as he could in twenty-four hours, he would just disappear into the vastness of the oceans until he found a small harbour that he was happy to call home. It was a pretty sketchy plan at best, but it appeared to be a more realistic option than the original one. Moving to the location of choice for most of Europe's fugitives from justice, while an international warrant for his arrest was being pursued, didn't stand up to any degree of scrutiny. Harry was also enthusiastic and pointed out that this would solve the problem of what to do with the yacht. They didn't really want to leave it bobbing about just off their landing point in France. Terry said that he would remove the radar reflector temporarily to hide the location where the others disembarked, and this was taken as confirmation that James's Plan B was no longer just a front runner.

All things considered they seemed to have a plan which, while far from ideal, appeared to be fit for purpose. They would have been surprised to know that Henry, who had been uncharacteristically quiet through their deliberations, had reservations which remained unspoken, deep reservations. Loose ends were as dangerous as loose talk; time bombs waiting to explode. The chain of events which had led them to their present predicament had all started with Shorty Clarke's loose talk, the loose end that Chris Wilson had felt compelled to eradicate. Henry had no doubt that Terry was as big a potential threat to them as Shorty Clarke had been to the members of the Ripper Gang.

The following day they rose early and Harry cooked his signature full English breakfast. By nine o'clock they were ready for the busy day that lay ahead of them. Tomorrow they were leaving England for the last time and sailing to France with only the cases they had brought with them and a random Chinese vase. Terry, however, would be packing for a much longer trip. The fortune that they had left Spain for had eluded them and their futures were less secure than they had ever been. James had suggested that sailing to Spain might be a more sensible option, but Terry wouldn't countenance landing them anywhere other than Northern France. He was the sailor so there wasn't really any alternative.

Terry left immediately with Harry and drove into Brighampton. He headed for the bank to remove as much cash from his accounts as possible. Any attempt to evade suspicion was irrelevant at this point. After the bank and building societies, he would hit the second hand shops and then the pawn shop which he had never entered before. Finally, he would sell the car for whatever he could get for it. There were two second-hand dealerships in the town so he was hoping he would get a more reasonable price than if the small town had only the one, as could easily have been the case. He had a feeling that getting paid in cash might prove problematic.

Harry was heading straight to the hardware shop to buy the paint and brushes necessary to turn The Lady Carmel into The Silver Sun of Poole. His expertise was in designing t-shirts but he was the only handyman in the group.

James and Henry continued to sanitise Barton Cottage leaving not a fingerprint, and with luck no D.N.A., in the building. It was a tall order but they would give it their best shot. By eight o'clock they were ready to leave the following morning. They all wore the plastic gloves normally used for checking engine oil levels which Terry had procured from the garage in town. They ate a simple salad and waited for the Nine O'clock News.

The Finnegan's Field riot and the mysterious deaths of a gang of burglars in the Hayden Gallery on the same night were only superseded by a foiled terrorist attack in Birmingham. However, the robbers were not yet named and Shorty Clarke's tattoo remained unreported. They heaved a collective sigh of relief and downed a few beers before heading to bed.

The Morning News informed them that a police update was imminent and that Chief Constable Stanley Bryant and Chief Superintendent Donovan would be holding a press conference at 2 p.m. They intended to listen to that broadcast from the English Channel.

The sea was choppy and the sky was grey. The sail flapped noisily and seagulls flew over the boat screaming loudly. They turned the volume up to max to counter the din around them, and huddled round the radio listening intently to the press conference. The police investigation was apparently progressing satisfactorily. The deceased burglars had been positively identified as The Ripper Gang by matching their D.N.A. to that found at the scene of several burglaries and they would be appealing for help from the public once the family of the last member had been informed of his death. It appeared that they were on holiday and were not expected to be informed until later on that day. A further update would then follow.

Once again Lady Luck seemed to be smiling on them and a round of beers was proposed and seconded. However, there had been no mention of a stolen vase, confirming Henry's assertion that there had never been a robbery. Terry's suggestion that the vase be chucked overboard as it had brought them nothing but bad luck was ignored, but he seemed troubled and when he spoke his voice shook with emotion.

'I honestly wish I'd never met you lot. Not because I don't like you. It's just that you've brought me nothing but trouble and the prospect of unrelenting grief in the future. That is if I have a future. I was happy with my cottage and my boat, if a bit strapped for cash. Look at me now. A fugitive from the law heading to God knows where in a small boat which you described as a floating caravan. One thing I will promise you though. Whatever the future holds, your part in this is safe with me. My lips are sealed and will remain so. I may have lost everything else but I will retain my honour. Honour among thieves,' he added, but there was no trace of humour in his voice or of a smile on his lips.

Once again Terry could be relied upon to dampen the mood and after assuring him, without much conviction, that things had a way of working out, everyone retreated into their own thoughts.

At eight o'clock in the evening they were sailing steadily towards a remote part of the coast which Terry was very familiar with. The occasional car on the coastal road could be seen clearly and Henry sat on the deck and watched them in the early evening light. He knew that he was heading towards an uncertain future but he'd been there before and he felt a mixture of relief and contentment. He'd be seeing dad again shortly. He was going home.

Terry dropped anchor in a small bay which he obviously knew well. It was deserted and even the cars driving along the coastal road were hidden from view. It was time to get their suitcases into the dinghy. A few minutes later Terry started the engine and they headed for the beach. James and Harry were the first to roll up their trousers and make their way ashore. As Henry got out of the dinghy he turned to Terry with a broad smile.

'Good luck Terry. I don't expect our paths will cross again but I do believe you when you say that, come what may, you won't drop us in it. I've made you a flask of coffee. It can't be easy when you're sailing on your own.' He smiled, 'You'll have to put your own milk and sugar in it.'

'Thanks Henry.' Terry sounded genuinely touched. 'Anything that helps me stay awake at the wheel is appreciated.'

Henry turned and lowered himself into the water. He liked Terry. As a matter of fact he liked Terry a lot. Not a bad bone in his body. He felt a sense of sadness he hadn't experienced since the night he first left Winkford, but this time he didn't look back.

Jack was parked a couple of hundred yards along the beach. He had watched them coming ashore, trousers rolled up and holding their suitcases above the water. James, who was carrying the sack containing the vase, was struggling a bit. Jack strode quickly towards them as they walked up the beach. He took the sack from James and carried on down to Henry. Henry greeted him with a beaming smile, and this time it was genuine.

That evening they booked themselves into a small hotel and ate at a bistro overlooking the sea. Jack brought them up to date with the police investigation and informed them that the members of the Ripper Gang had been poisoned; a massive overdose of powerful sleeping pills in their coffee. With James and Harry staring accusingly at him, Henry decided that this was the time to come clean on his role in their deaths. Their reaction went from shock to dismay and finally alarm. It slowly dawned on James and Harry that they could now be portrayed as accomplices in a murder inquiry. Henry explained that he had merely been attempting to fulfil his part of the enterprise. He would have accomplished it very satisfactorily if Shorty Clarke had turned out to be short and Terry had provided a separate flask for him as agreed. The important thing was that they weren't connected to the attempted robbery or the ensuing

176

deaths, so they didn't have to worry about a future murder charge. Somewhat reassured, they headed to the nearest bar in a more subdued state of mind. It was small and quiet with only a few locals watching a football match on T.V. They ordered a round of beers and updated Jack on their experiences in England. He shook his head in amazement. He had been expecting a story but this beggared belief. It sounded more like the plot of a trashy novel than the real life experiences of his son and the friends he knew so well.

His one concern was Terry. James and Harry showed their agreement by their awkward glances and total lack of comment on the subject. Henry, however, had no such concerns. He was confident that Terry would be as good as his word and take his secrets to the grave. Anymore talk of death by coffee would be ill judged at best. He spoke with a conviction that was as reassuring as it was improbable. After a few more beers the evening drew to a close. It had been a troubling evening which had followed days of stress and anxiety. The decision was unanimous that the journey back should be relaxed and unhurried. In short, it should be enjoyed. The following days included long lunches and small bars before retiring to that evening's hotel. On Friday afternoon they drove into the beautiful city of Carcassonne and spent the next day as tourists, soaking up its medieval grandeur.

On Sunday morning their car crossed the border into Spain without the customs officials giving it as much as a second glance. Twenty-four hours later their reception might have been very different. The Ming Vase theft was about to become breaking news in England. Its recovery and the apprehending of the thieves responsible for its theft became the overriding concern of the Commissioner of Police of the Metropolis who was asked by the Home Secretary to personally oversee the operation. Unbeknown to Henry, Harry, and James, a massive police operation was being launched with the sole purpose of bringing them to justice for the heist of the Ming vase and first degree murder.

Chapter Twenty-Three

As they crossed the border and entered Spain, Sophie Lawson entered the Winkford police station and walked purposefully to the desk. She gave her name, showed her I.D. card, and waited while the desk sergeant made an internal call. PC Winch was expecting the call. She opened the station safe and retrieved the key to the cabinet housing the Ming Vase. After exchanging a few pleasantries she handed the key to Miss Lawson who signed for it and then escorted her across the road to the Hayden Gallery.

The two security guards on the door made a point of scrutinising her I.D. and smiled as they unlocked the door for her. Sophie Lawson loved her job, and in her eight year association with the National Gallery she had never been so closely involved with such a prestigious and popular exhibition. The extension of the exhibition at the Haydon Gallery by a week in order to cash in on its unexpected notoriety had been a resounding success, and it was hoped that the surge in interest would follow its now extended tour to its last five destinations.

She walked slowly around the exhibition making sure that the exhibits were being wrapped by the specialised removal company with due diligence,, before walking towards the glass cabinet which held pride of place in the centre of the exhibition. No one was going to open that particular cabinet without a key. This was a level of toughened glass only found in the most secure premises. As she carefully removed the vase she immediately felt that something was wrong. It seemed heavier than she remembered. She turned it over and read the inscription on the base in horror. In perfect English was the stamp.

MADE IN CHINA

The Home Secretary was made aware of the robbery that evening and he phoned the Prime Minister immediately. The P.M. seemed remarkably relaxed about the news and asked if it was true that the quality of Chinese goods was improving. The Home Secretary, whose recent speech about the ability of police forces to absorb government spending cuts had dwelt largely on the recent success of the Winkford constabulary, didn't find it amusing. His next call was to Chief Constable Stanley Bryant.

Sarah Bryant was enjoying a lovely evening. Her husband was guest of honour at the Winkford Conservative Club's annual ball. With the Ripper Gang removed from circulation permanently, a result which the highly vocal hang them and flog them wing of the party could only have dreamt of, and the Chinese Exhibition being extended to an additional three locations amid a frenzy of press interest, he was attaining celebrity status far beyond the confines of his policing region. Presently, he would give a short speech on law and order to a guaranteed standing ovation. Could it get any better?

Stanley Bryant had a knot in his stomach. He disliked public speaking. He was running through his prompts one last time before he stood up to deliver the speech which had kept him up for most of the previous night, when DI Jones approached him at speed.

'Can you switch on your mobile Sir? The Home Secretary wants to speak to you and he says it's urgent.'

Stanley took the mobile from his jacket pocket. He felt a sense of foreboding and the knot in his stomach was tightening.

As they drove into Spain, blissfully unaware of developments in England, the mood in the car lightened perceptibly. Only Henry seemed to become more withdrawn. They were heading towards a reunion with Walter Krosney and Henry was not sure how amiable their reception might be. Unaware that the vase they were transporting to Marbella wasn't a worthless fake, there didn't appear to be any good news to mitigate the death of Chris Wilson. When he had sent Henry to England in order to kill an unstable thief, he had expected him to do just that. Just that, Henry thought ruefully. Killing one of his business associates, who also happened to be a good friend, was not in the job description. It was dawning on

Henry that going off script could have consequences. After travelling at a leisurely pace through quiet and picturesque countryside, much of it on secondary roads, they finally arrived in Marbella on Wednesday evening. Jack dropped them off at their respective apartments where they freshened up before meeting up again at The Fusion Bar for a final evening with just the four of them. They reminisced on their English adventure over pizza, washed down with cold beers. Henry rang Walter as they were leaving to inform him of their arrival in Marbella.

'It's great to hear from you. We were beginning to worry. Walter's voice oozed concern and just a hint of menace. I'll meet you at the Honolulu Bar for lunch tomorrow. Have you got the vase?'

'We've got a vase,' Henry replied in a voice so inscrutable that even Ling Junsheng would have been proud of it. Explanations could wait until tomorrow.

Over a light lunch Walter brought them up to date with events in England. The vase in James' apartment was almost certainly the original Ming Vase and Mr Junshen was ecstatic at having achieved a lifelong ambition. They were richer to the tune of two hundred and fifty thousand pounds each. Mr Junshen would retain Terry's share in case he eventually made contact at some point in the future. He felt that this was entirely possible. It appeared that Terry's boat had been abandoned in the English Channel. Initially suicide was suspected but with the Ming Vase still not recovered, and its value giving the directors of Lloyds of London sleepless nights, conspiracy theories abounded.

'A warrant has been issued for his arrest,' Walter informed them. 'The French police are heavily involved in the search as that is where he is believed to have headed. He is familiar with the coastal areas in particular. He is now being compared to Lord Lucan,' Walter chuckled. 'I expect he'll be sighted in Australia and South America by the end of the week.'

More likely Beachy Head, thought Henry, but only a smile broke his lips.

Walter's mood became more subdued as he then brought them up to speed on the police investigation which was being ramped up significantly on a daily basis. The Commissioner of Police of the Metropolis had taken personal responsibility for overseeing the investigation at the request of the Home Secretary. However, due to his involvement in previous attempts to apprehend the Ripper Gang, Chief Constable Stanley Bryant had been seconded to Scotland Yard in order to take charge of the day to day running of the investigation and liaise with the media on their progress.

'It's been assumed by the police, the press, and the citizens of England, that the bodies who were discovered in the Haydon Gallery were the result of a falling out among thieves. However, the Ripper Gang are acquiring celebrity status in death, and appear to be admired rather than deplored by the bulk of the British public. It's not going down well with the police and the legal establishment. If this investigation ends up at your door I guarantee that they'll lock you up and throw the keys away.

Henry assured him that they had left England secure in the knowledge that there was no link between them and the Ripper Gang and he had no doubt that this was still the case. James and Harry nodded in agreement but couldn't hide their concern. Walter's enquiry as to what had happened to Chris and the rest of the gang held the unspoken allegation that Henry had been dreading. His simple assertion that it had been unintentional and was honestly and deeply regretted appeared, to his surprise, to be enough to allay any misgivings that Walter might have had. He promised to acquaint him of the details at a more appropriate time. As the lunchtime update was coming to a close Walter took the opportunity to pull Henry to one side.

'Mr Junsheng was impressed by the part you played in the acquisition of his vase. He admires your professionalism and would pay handsomely to avail himself of your expertise in the future.' Walter suggested they meet the following day to discuss 'things' in more detail.

'Here's as good a place as any.'

A one o'clock lunch at the Honolulu Bar was agreed.

Henry considered Mr Junsheng's offer of future employment. The coal mining industry was not one that he had ever associated with Machiavellian intrigue and assassination. However, on the way home he paid the local linen store a visit and purchased a pack of pillows.

Henry arrived at the Honolulu Bar early and was sitting at a table by the window when Walter entered the bar. He acknowledged the barman with a wave and a beaming smile. His jovial mood remained as he strode across the floor towards Henry with a pint of beer in each hand. They both said 'cheers' in unison before savouring the amber nectar. As they returned their glasses to the table Henry spoke first.

'So what do I need to know with regard to my blossoming relationship with Mr Ling Junsheng? I presume that I won't be dealing with him directly and that you'll be the middleman. Nice work if you can get it.' Henry chuckled.

'Oh you'll deal with him through me.'

Walter spoke quietly but the good humour had been erased from his expression. His mood underwent a total transformation. The sympathetic listener of yesterday was replaced by a steely coolness and as he spoke his tone conveyed a subtle threat.

'I was the middleman between Mr Junsheng and the Ripper Gang which was an all-consuming occupation at the time. When Chris approached me for help with his 'Shorty' problem I wasn't able to offer a solution. I don't associate with murderers, never have, and didn't ever expect to.' He paused. 'And then I met you. I had no real expectation that you would accept the offer. When you did I felt that warm glow of satisfaction that accompanies the ability to help a good friend. I was able to inform Chris that I had found an assassin who could in no way be connected with him. I assumed you would just shoot him. Uncomplicated and requiring no particular expertise. Anyone can pull a trigger and provided you are close enough you can't really miss. But you no more knew how to procure a gun than I knew how to contact a career assassin. When Chris told me you intended to overpower Shorty Clarke and then

182

suffocate him with a pillow I was seriously concerned. At first I wrote you off as a mad fantasist.'

Walter paused. He looked grim

'I was right about one thing. You are mad. However not mad like the patient on a psychiatric ward who thinks he's Elvis. No, you're scary mad. You could be a character in a Stephen King novel, an inoffensive and insignificant little fat man who kills everyone who gets in his way; and without a shred of remorse.'

He looked Henry straight in the eye. 'I've taken out a personal protection plan and your future is now linked to my good health.'

Henry was genuinely shocked. 'You don't seriously think I would kill you?'

'Don't seriously think you would kill me. I think your wife is lucky to be locked up at Her Majesty's pleasure. So far she's the only person who seems to have escaped your self-preservation policy to date. Well I'm the second.' He was starting to lose his composure and his hand began to shake.

Good God, Henry thought. He's afraid of me. He really rather liked the feeling. This must be what it feels like to be a Partner he thought. In truth he liked the feeling a lot.

Walter pulled himself together.

'My solicitor has a letter to be opened and acted upon in the event of my death. It details everything I know about your murderous career to date. Don't bother coming to my funeral. You'll be arrested and your future prospects, if that happens, don't bear thinking about.'

He finished his beer and was suddenly transformed back to the unflappable cheery person that Henry knew so well, or thought he did. He offered his thoughts on the political situation in England, commented on the weather, and left an incredulous Henry with the same beaming smile with which he had entered the bar.

Henry ordered another beer and considered the situation in which he now found himself. As well as being a problem, Walter was also an integral part of his future employment by Ling Junsheng. God it was complicated. However he was sure a plan to remove the problem would be expedient and could do no harm. Henry had seen Walter coming out of a solicitor's office some time ago. It was on the opposite side of the road from Fanny's Emporium and Henry had been researching handcuffs and alternative restraints at the time. He didn't know anyone who had more than one solicitor and was confident that Walter would be no different. It wasn't the most salubrious of areas which was surprising, but no doubt Walter had his reasons for employing such a small and unassuming firm of solicitors. The trick would be to break into the solicitor's office, remove the letter, and then introduce Walter to the grim reaper on the same evening. Walter appeared to be in good health so for once he wasn't up against the clock. However it would be prudent to prepare a contingency plan.

At nine o'clock the following evening Henry was standing outside Fanny's Emporium, staring at the solicitor's office across the street. It wasn't just small, it was small and shabby. He crossed the road. Through the window he could see a reception area with a desk on which there was a phone and a monitor, a couple of filing cabinets, and a bookcase. There were three doors on the back wall, the one on the left marked 'Servicios'. He presumed the other two must be the offices. Durand and Moreau solicitors appeared to consist of just two lawyers, Durand and Moreau, and a receptionist. The window surround and the door would both benefit from a fresh coat of paint. He was convinced that any alarm system would be very basic but he wouldn't be surprised if they didn't have one. Apart from Walter's incriminating letter he doubted if there was anything in the offices worth stealing. A locked filing cabinet was probably the extent of their security. There were apartments above all the shops and offices on the street and most seemed occupied, but they had their curtains drawn. None of the occupants would be surveying the street which was deserted, bereft of pedestrians and traffic.

He arranged a visit to Durand and Moreau, ostensibly to discuss a house purchase in the near future, but actually to assess their security. The receptionist was a homely and pleasant woman with a dress sense bordering on severe. Mr

Durand was a genial man, softly spoken and composed. Henry guessed he was probably in his late fifties. He didn't meet Mr Moreau. The office was old, almost Dickensian, and there was a musty smell which he presumed to be the odour of old books. It was an unusual choice of solicitor for a property developer. He left feeling confident that there was no alarm system and that their security consisted of a large and quite substantial cupboard with a lock. The front window didn't appear to be double glazed but he still had traumatic memories of the last time he'd entered a building through a glass window. The door had a deadlock but he was confident that this could easily be cut out of the wooden door with the aid of the appropriate drill accessories. A couple of days later he scoured the neighbourhood for CCTV cameras but could find none.

Stanley Bryant was happy to lead the police investigation into the theft of the Ming vase and the death of four members of the Ripper Gang, but was less comfortable with the PR which appeared to be a significant part of his remit. He was instructed to hold a weekly televised press conference in order to keep both Press and public updated on their progress, and this was way outside his comfort zone. He became increasingly anxious as each of those press conferences approached.

This was his third weekly update and he felt the same level of anxiety as he had experienced during the lead up to the first one. The initial briefing had gone remarkably well. The assembled journalists had listened intently as Stanley gave an upbeat assessment of their progress to date. They had established a link with Portugal and South Korea and it was becoming apparent that the Ripper Gang was part of a much larger international crime syndicate. In order to follow up those leads a couple of experienced detectives from Scotland Yard had flown out to Tavira in Portugal earlier that morning, and two more were booked on a flight to Incheon in South Korea that afternoon. He had wrapped up the briefing with confidence and composure. They had hit the ground running and he anticipated being able to report some tangible progress the following week.

The following day Henry read the articles which accompanied the dramatic newspaper headlines with increasing concern. He had played no part in setting up the fake entertainment company in Portugal and he had no idea how thorough the precautions taken by Mr Junsheng to conceal the identity of James and Harry had been. Could an exhaustive investigation by skilled sleuths connect them to the theft of the Ming vase and the murders which had accompanied it? He was worried and awaited the next update with increasing anxiety.

The address in Portugal of Entretenimento Internacional turned out to be a derelict building which was due to be demolished as soon as the planning application for its replacement was approved. The police in Tavira were eager to assist them but could find no connection between the deceased members of the Ripper Gang and their town. Enquiries at the towns tourist information centre, hotels, bars, and restaurants, were unproductive. Entretenimento Internacional's bank a/c had been opened in Tavira by a small Chinese woman with a thick Chinese accent. The detectives asked the Assistant Branch Manager who had set up the account, and spoke perfect English, to describe her, and he told them that she had looked Chinese. On being asked if he could provide a more detailed description he explained that they all looked the same. His demeanour suggested that he thought he was stating the obvious. The detectives in Incheon fared no better. The press had dwelt heavily on the fact that it was the most violent city in South Korea and their readers were led to anticipate the exposing of a sinister criminal syndicate whose malevolent tentacles spread around the world. However, the phone and e-mail address used to organise the Finnegan's Field music festival were both registered to a one bedroom apartment on the outskirts of the city which had been the home of its elderly resident for almost fifty years. It came as no surprise that she only spoke Korean. While she did possess a mobile phone it was used sparingly and almost exclusively to receive calls from her family. It had never been used to contact anyone outside the city. After five frustrating minutes, their Korean interpreter gave up trying to explain to her what an e-mail was. The

186

detectives had returned from both locations a few days later with no hint of a link to the Ripper Gang.

The next update had been a much more subdued affair and Stanley quickly regretted raising expectations a week earlier. When questions were invited from the floor a reporter pointed out that a simple phone call to the local police authorities in Tavira and Incheon would have accomplished the same results. It was an observation that Stanley couldn't refute. His justification for flying detectives half way round the world on a wild goose chase was that, while the leads now appeared to be carefully contrived blind alleys, they were leads, and every lead had to be followed up. The fact that they led to Portugal and South Korea did however support the supposition that the gang had international connections.

As he began his third update, Stanley viewed the rows of reporters in front of him with as much apprehension as on the previous two briefings, aware that they were unlikely to be impressed by the change of direction that the investigation was taking. He did his best to sound optimistic as he brought them up to speed and informed them that they were now concentrating their enquiries on the family and acquaintances of the deceased burglars. While they had no new leads as yet, he declared that they remained hopeful, and asked that any member of the public who had information on the known members of the Ripper Gang come forward. A dedicated phone line had been made available to facilitate this. With real apprehension, he asked if there were any questions.

The first reporter to put a question to Stanley looked far from impressed and asked what every journalist in the room was thinking.

'Is that it?'

Stanley chose to ignore him and offered the floor to a journalist from one of the tabloids. If he was hoping to get a less challenging question he was to be disappointed. He was asked why he thought an international criminal gang appeared to be concentrating their efforts within a fifty mile radius of Winkford.

Stanley was a competent Chief Constable but he found himself floundering in a string of tough questions being delivered by an unsympathetic audience in an increasingly combative manner; questions to which he had no convincing answers because there didn't seem to be any. He could only reiterate that the Finnegan's Field festival had been organised from Portugal and the phone and e-mail address of Entretenimento Internacional were registered in South Korea. Those were facts that couldn't be disputed. His observation that the case was not just baffling, it was bizarre, became the dramatic headline in several papers the following day.As the press conference progressed from being uncomfortable to becoming embarrassing, Stanley brought it to an abrupt end by taking no more questions and leaving.

A few days later a spokesman for Scotland Yard announced that there would no longer be a press conference each week as it had been decided to give updates as and when there were developments to report. In due course the investigation was downgraded substantially, although it remained open. Stanley Bryant returned quietly to Winkford and the dedicated phone line was rerouted to a police call centre in Croydon.

As the weeks became months and Walter returned to his easygoing ways, with never as much as a mention of their acrimonious exchange in the Honolulu Bar, Henry began to put the problem to the back of his mind. He hadn't entrusted anyone else with an account of Walter's threat to him as a result of Chris Wilson's death, not even Jack. Walter had reverted to being an amusing and amiable friend and Henry ceased to dwell on the possible consequences of his damning letter sitting in a solicitor's office. The Surrey Echo had ceased to make any comment on the police investigation and it was no longer the dominant story in the tabloids, although they did go back to it occasionally to question the competence of the police. He followed any coverage of the investigation by buying a selection of English Newspapers every day, and was encouraged by what little news there was. The police enquiries were not going well and reports on their progress had deteriorated from unfavourable comment to scathing criticism. Their investigations appeared to be concentrating solely on friends or acquaintances of the murdered men and were leading nowhere. Henry's natural optimism rose to the surface again. With every passing day the possibility a breakthrough in the case seemed to be receding further, his financial situation had been transformed, although he had heard no more from Ling Junsheng, and he was settling contentedly into his expat lifestyle.

Camille Martin was about to change all that.

It was Sunday. It was a beautiful day. The weather was warm and sultry. Camille Martin was a very beautiful girl, as warm and sultry as the weather. Those two facts were to bring Henry's life into crisis again.

When Camille got out of bed that morning she went straight to the window and opened the curtains. As the sunlight streamed into her bedroom she didn't know what she would be wearing that day, but she did know that it wouldn't be very much.

As Louis Dubois drove down a quiet road in Marbella a couple of hours later his eyes rested on the beautiful girl walking along the pavement towards him. Camille Martin was wearing a short skirt, a low cut top, and sunglasses. As she strolled up the street she presented a greater hazard to traffic than any blind corner or adverse camber. Louis hardly noticed the sunglasses. Unfortunately, that was all he didn't notice and he was transfixed by the vision walking towards him. He didn't see Walter Krosney's car until he hit it, and that was the last thing he ever saw. Walter had no time to avoid the car which suddenly veered across the road towards him. The emergency services arrived in an impressively short period of time and half an hour later Walter was hooked up to a drip in intensive care.

It was James who rang Jack and Henry with the bad news a few hours later and they immediately made their way to the hospital. James, Harry, and a couple of Walter's acquaintances whom they didn't know, were already there. James gave them the bad news. Walter was in a critical condition. He might pull through but it was far from certain. The next forty-eight hours would be crucial. There seemed little point in hanging around so after about an hour they all left. Jack, Harry, and James all headed for the Honolulu Bar but Henry headed back to his apartment. He needed to be on his own as he considered the predicament he now found himself in. He sat at the kitchen table and slowly supped a cold beer. The need for a solution was pressing.

Henry was suddenly up against the clock again. The hard earned lifestyle he had achieved was in danger of being snatched from him by an imminent death for which he was in no way responsible. He felt aggrieved, annoyed, and anxious. Of course, Walter might pull through. There was no way of knowing. Well actually there was. Henry would have to make sure that he didn't. If he ever became connected to the Ripper Gang he could look forward to a very long prison sentence in an establishment where the majority of his companions would be men who resembled Shorty Clarke. This was the time to remove the problem.

He would have to break into a small office with no alarm system, located on a quiet road with no CCTV cameras. He would have to locate an envelope, which would undoubtedly be filed in alphabetical order, in an office cabinet which had a rudimentary lock. He would then have to despatch an unconscious man to the afterlife in a building which was literally full of his chosen weapon. He wouldn't have to come armed with a pillow. He was walking into an armoury. Henry's optimism and confidence was never greater. To a man with his C.V. this would be a walk in the park.

Henry Hetherington-Busby, the quiet and unassuming accountant from Winkford, caught sight of his reflection in the mirror opposite. The man who smiled back at him looked confident to the point of arrogance. The smile became a broad grin. What could possibly go wrong?

Chapter Twenty Four

Henry looked at his watch. It was ten to one and there had been light rain for about twenty minutes. From the shelter of the shop doorway across the road from Durand and Moreau he could see that the street was still deserted. Clouds blocked out any moonlight which might have provided street lighting. He scoured the windows of the apartments above the shops but every curtain was closed and no lights were on. Their occupants of Calle de Carlos Bernardo were all securely tucked up in bed.

He still felt the sense of unease which had begun to descend on him as he prepared to put his plan into action. This was phase one, and it was the easy part. Phase two, in the hospital, would be less straight forward than it had first appeared. It would be one hundred per cent improvisation and that was causing him some concern. He pulled up his coat collar, picked up the rucksack, and walked quickly across the road to the offices of Durand and Moreau. A deathly silence seemed to have fallen over the street with even the light rain making no sound. Henry took the electric saw out of the haversack. It had seemed reasonably quiet in his kitchen. Now he wasn't quite so sure. However, the wooden door wasn't just old, it was old and rotten, its condition disguised by numerous layers of paint. He cut the lock out with ease and stepped into the reception area. Fortune favours the brave he thought as he entered the office of Mr Durrand. He'd expected the door to be locked but it wasn't even closed. He laughed out loud. No security problems here then. He switched on his torch and shone it on to the large wooden cabinet which undoubtedly housed Walter Krosney's malicious and damning letter. The beam moved quickly past the lock on the cabinet doors and down through the drawers below. On the floor there were two large bowls, one containing a few pieces of meat while the other was full of water.

As their significance dawned on Henry a vicious growl broke the silence and alerted him to the fact that security had entered the room. He instantly recognised the musty smell in the offices and it wasn't old books.

He turned to see a hundred and ten pounds of Rottweiler. Its tail wasn't wagging and its teeth were bared and dripping with saliva. As Henry stared in terror at the venomous fangs of his nightmares he froze, rooted to the spot. The dog leapt at him and he crashed to the wooden floor under its weight. Just before he drifted out of consciousness he thought he heard a familiar voice.

'Get a grip little man; get a grip.'

When Henry came too it was a gradual process. He felt groggy and was initially unaware of where he was, but very aware of the pain in his left shoulder. When he moved the pain in his leg and ankle became apparent. However, it was the sight of his left hand which shocked him out of his stupor. He quickly grasped the severity of his situation. He remembered the Rottweiler, but it was no longer in the room. It must have got bored with the unconscious body on the floor.

Just as well, thought Henry as he looked again at his injured left hand. The skin at the base of his thumb had been pulled off to the bone and three of his fingers appeared to be badly bitten. While his hand was not as painful as his shoulder or ankle, it was obviously in the most need of attention. He remained quite still. There was neither sight nor sound of the dog, and he wanted to keep it that way while he considered his options, if indeed he had any. If this was the end of his criminal career it had been a short one. Distinguished, but short.

So what were his options?

The dog had disappeared for the moment but it couldn't have gone far; there wasn't far to go. The gentle Mr Durand was unlikely to own a Rottweiler. He was probably Mr Moreau's dog and there would no doubt be a dog basket in his office. While he remained silent the dog was unlikely to disturb him, but he needed medical attention and he needed it quickly. Just lying there wasn't an option. Furthermore, the incriminating letter from Walter Krosney was as tantalisingly close as he was to catastrophe. He'd had his fair share of good luck along with the bad. Would lady luck smile on him one more time?

He hadn't entrusted anyone else with the account of Walter's threat to him, and he certainly hadn't told anyone of his homicidal plans for this evening. Given his recent history he could easily acquire a reputation for casually bumping off his friends whenever they became problematic; not a recipe for winning popularity competitions. Blood was seeping slowly but persistently from his injured hand with no sign of clotting, and a crimson pool was spreading sluggishly across the floor. If he didn't get his hand stitched quickly, Mr Durand and Mr Moreau might find a corpse on their reception room floor when they opened up in the morning. However, if he phoned the emergency services and informed them that medical assistance was urgently required at this address, he could think of no scenario in which he wouldn't be taken to hospital and then onward to a police cell. There had to be another option.

Henry prepared himself mentally, and slowly started to pick himself up from the floor ever so quietly. That was until he put his weight on to his injured ankle. He gave an involuntary scream. It was now a race against the Rottweiler and the consequence of losing was too dreadful to contemplate. With all of his weight on to his good right foot, he threw himself against the door. As he heard the catch click he felt the crushing sense of despair turn to jubilant relief. It seemed to counter the excruciating pain in his ankle. He leant against the door and waited until the dog had stopped growling. In the silence of the night it seemed very loud and he was suddenly aware of the occupants of the apartment above. He could only hope that they were sleeping soundly and the insulation in the ceiling was of a better standard than the timber in the door frame. It only heightened his awareness that the need for action was pressing. Retrieving his mobile phone from his left hand pocket was to prove a task of Herculean proportions. He phoned Jack.

Jack was shaken as he listened to Henry's plea for help.

He was worried, horrified, and initially at a loss for words, but after Henry had finished explaining his predicament, he told him that he would be with him shortly.

'You were going to kill Walter,' was his only other comment. He sounded bewildered and appalled.

Jack entered the building about half an hour later brandishing a fire extinguisher as though it was a shotgun. As the Rottweiler sprang at him he pressed the trigger and it was thrown back by a wall of pressurised foam. Confused and disorientated it ran in panic to the safety of Mr Moreau's office and he had merely to shut the door behind it. He helped Henry to get up from the floor on his good leg, pulled his arm over his shoulder, and carried him out of the building. After helping him on to a bench which was a short distance away, he walked to his car which was parked at the end of the road. As he drove back to Henry he scrutinized the apartment above the offices of Durand and Moreau, but, like all the other apartments in the street, it was in darkness, its occupants seemingly undisturbed by the canine mugging which had taken place one floor below them. After helping Henry into the passenger seat, he started the engine and headed for the hospital.

'You look terrible. God alone knows how you're going to explain the damage to your hand. I've never seen anything like it, and I haven't led a sheltered life.'

The pain in Henry's ankle and hand had subsided a little but he was in no mood to engage in conversation. He told Jack he'd explain everything in more detail later, but as Jack turned into the hospital grounds he took a large brown envelope out of his coat pocket with his right hand and placed it on Jack's lap.

'Have a read of that when you get home.'

'What is it?' Jack asked him.

Somehow, Henry raised a smile. 'Walter's suicide note.'

On this occasion his story of being attacked by a Rottweiler while out for a late night stroll was consistent with his injuries and his wounded hand raised a lot of sympathy, but no suspicion, as it was patched up at the hospital.

Walter Krosney came up trumps and ensured that his unresolved issues with Henry were put to rest once and for all by dying three days later. Henry didn't attend the funeral, citing his obvious injuries as the reason for his absence. Even though he had rescued the incriminating letter from the offices of Durand and Moreau, he felt nervous about being there, and was glad to have a convincing reason for not making an appearance. Walter was quickly forgotten, other than the occasional reminiscence, and Henry settled back into his old routine, with his life revolving around the usual group of friends at the Honolulu bar. The break in at Durand and Moreau had merited a column in the local paper for one day, and, while his hand was noticeably scarred, it was now fully functional. As the weeks became months, the Pillow Case and all its possible ramifications faded from his thoughts. The sun was shining, the company was entertaining, and he was living the expat dream. The Winkford police seemed, and indeed were, a thousand miles away and concentrating on more recent and urgent cases.

Ten months had passed and Henry was sipping a cold beer on Jack's balcony. They had just returned from lunch at Hippo. The sun was shining and a cool breeze from the sea complemented its warmth perfectly. Henry was unusually quiet and Jack looked thoughtful.

'What's on your mind Henry, you haven't been yourself for days?'

'I suppose I've too much time on my hands; time to think about the future. Two hundred and fifty thousand pounds seemed a lot of money. It isn't really. Not with interest rates as they are. Not when you're my age. It'll last for a quite a few more years but there's another day of reckoning awaiting me. It isn't imminent but it is inevitable. It's a bit like having a terminal disease which isn't affecting you at present, but which will be as malignant as it is incurable. We're living a dream which can't be sustained Jack, and that day of reckoning will come.'

He looked Jack straight in the eye.

'I know your bank balance isn't as healthy as mine Jack, and your reserves won't last forever. I'll be your pension plan while I'm solvent but I don't see any more Ripper Gangs on the horizon. Do you?'

Jack took a pause before replying. 'There's no point in worrying about what might happen years from now. We might end up like Walter Krosney and all that worry will have been for nothing.'

'You're right.'

Henry smiled and raised his glass, but his smile lacked conviction. It was six months later that he got the phone call. He answered his mobile with a certain amount of trepidation. He gave out his phone number sparingly. The voice that spoke to him was both educated and corporate.

'Good afternoon Mr Busby-Hetherington, my name is Oliver. I am an associate of Mr Zhou and he is a friend and associate of Mr Junsheng. He has a problem and Mr Junsheng has advised him that you may be able to help him solve it. Mr Junsheng has not forgotten how well you served him when he had a similar problem in the past. Would you be interested?'

There was a short pause.

'He would be generous.'

A beaming smile broke Henry's face as he felt a weight lifting from his shoulders. He'd done his apprenticeship. He'd made mistakes as he'd honed his skills and learnt his trade, but now he was the real deal, a true professional. Would Mr Zhou be his last client obtained by recommendation? Only time would tell. He could be embarking on a new career. He considered what the future might hold. It could be much more interesting than accountancy, a lot more exciting than accountancy, and considerably more lucrative than accountancy.

'Hello Oliver. You can tell Mr Zhou that I'm interested.'

Printed in Great Britain
by Amazon

63165859R00119